AFTER THE FIRE

Rose Marie Ferris

A CANDLELIGHT ECSTASY ROMANCE™

Published by
Dell Publishing Co., Inc.
1 Dag Hammarskjold Plaza
New York, New York 10017

Dell ® TM 681510, Dell Publishing Co., Inc.

Candlelight Ecstasy Romance™ is a trademark of
Dell Publishing Co., Inc., New York, New York.

ISBN: 0-440-10036-4

Printed in the United States of America

First printing—January 1982

A Candlelight
Ecstasy Romance ™

"HOW CAN IT BE SEDUCTION WHEN I WANT YOU SO MUCH," SHE WHISPERED.

"You're too young to know what you want," he countered dismissively.

She saw the conflicting emotions in his expression as desire battled reason, as need warred with caution, and when she pressed her cheek to his chest, she heard the wild thudding of his heart.

Shamelessly she pleaded, "I don't require much space, and I wouldn't eat very much. It wouldn't cost you anything at all to keep me."

"Only my sanity," Adam muttered hoarsely.

In the next instant his arms crushed her to him, and his mouth was hard and demanding as it claimed the yielding softness of hers.

CANDLELIGHT ECSTASY ROMANCES™

1 THE TAWNY GOLD MAN, *Amii Lorin*
2 GENTLE PIRATE, *Jayne Castle*
3 THE PASSIONATE TOUCH, *Bonnie Drake*
4 THE SHADOWED REUNION, *Lillian Cheatham*
5 ONLY THE PRESENT, *Noelle Berry McCue*
6 LEAVES OF FIRE, FLAME OF LOVE, *Susan Chatfield*
7 THE GAME IS PLAYED, *Amii Lorin*
8 OCEAN OF REGRETS, *Noelle Berry McCue*
9 SURRENDER BY MOONLIGHT, *Bonnie Drake*
10 GENTLEMAN IN PARADISE, *Harper McBride*
11 MORGAN WADE'S WOMAN, *Amii Lorin*
12 THE TEMPESTUOUS LOVERS, *Suzanne Simmons*
13 THE MARRIAGE SEASON, *Sally Dubois*
14 THE HEART'S AWAKENING, *Valerie Ferris*
15 DESPERATE LONGINGS, *Frances Flores*
16 BESIEGED BY LOVE, *Maryann Young*
17 WAGERED WEEKEND, *Jayne Castle*
18 SWEET EMBER, *Bonnie Drake*
19 TENDER YEARNINGS, *Elaine Raco Chase*
20 THE FACE OF LOVE, *Anne N. Reisser*
21 LOVE'S ENCORE, *Rachel Ryan*
22 BREEZE OFF THE OCEAN, *Amii Lorin*
23 RIGHT OF POSSESSION, *Jayne Castle*
24 THE CAPTIVE LOVE, *Anne N. Reisser*
25 FREEDOM TO LOVE, *Sabrina Myles*
26 BARGAIN WITH THE DEVIL, *Jayne Castle*
27 GOLDEN FIRE, SILVER ICE, *Marisa de Zavala*
28 STAGES OF LOVE, *Beverly Sommers*
29 LOVE BEYOND REASON, *Rachel Ryan*
30 PROMISES TO KEEP, *Rose Marie Ferris*
31 WEB OF DESIRE, *Jean Hager*
32 SENSUOUS BURGUNDY, *Bonnie Drake*
33 DECEPTIVE LOVE, *Anne N. Reisser*

Dear Reader:

In response to your enthusiasm for Candlelight Ecstasy Romances™, we are now increasing the number of titles per month from three to four.

We are pleased to offer you sensuous novels set in America, depicting modern American women and men as they confront the provocative problems of a modern relationship.

Throughout the history of the Candlelight line, Dell has tried to maintain a high standard of excellence, to give you the finest in reading pleasure. It is now and will remain our most ardent ambition.

Editor
Candlelight Romances

AFTER THE FIRE

CHAPTER ONE

Shannon MacLeod shivered when the ruins of the ski lodge came into view. Despite the warmth of the late August sun she was touched by a cold frisson of foreboding. Braking sharply, she brought the Volkswagen to a stop at the side of the road.

The fire of seven years before had destroyed even the hickory trees from which Shagbark Inn derived its name. Their charred remains marked what had once been the perimeter of the cocktail lounge, but with the exception of a few decaying, fire-blackened beams, all that was left of the inn itself was the freestanding chimney of the great stone fireplace.

For more than five decades the fireplace had warmed the lobby, offering a cheery welcome to the inn's guests. Now the chimney pointed toward the sky like an accusatory finger, offering a grim memorial to the lodge and to generations of MacLeod family enterprise. According to Dr. Follensbee it would soon be a monument to her grandmother Agatha MacLeod as well.

Until this moment, however, Shannon hadn't begun to come to terms with that possibility.

Since the doctor's telephone call—was it only four days ago?—Shannon had been so preoccupied with preparations for her return home that the gravity of her grandmother's condition hadn't really penetrated. She had been shielded by the time and distance of separation and by the myriad requirements of settling her affairs in Minneapolis. Her deliberate concentration on superficialities was so complete that it had been this morning before she'd thought to contact Mr. Drexel, the principal, and inform him that she would be unable to teach first grade next term. She'd intentionally kept busy—packing, arranging to sublet her apartment and store most of her furniture—so that she'd have little time to think about her grandmother's illness.

Shannon was still shielded, for she'd had very little sleep the past few nights and she was numb with fatigue. Her gray eyes were amethyst-shadowed by weariness, but they were wide and unwavering as she stared at the ruins.

Shagbark Inn might not have been as luxurious as Eagles Nest, its nearest neighbor. It might not have been as inexpensive and convenient in its proximity to Galena as the Rainbow Ridge resort. But for more than fifty years it had been a local landmark.

Its location on towering palisades overlooking the Mississippi River had made its ski slopes the finest in northwestern Illinois, and it had a rustic quaintness that brought to mind a Currier & Ives lithograph. Its reputation as a family vacation spot had spread until it attracted a clientele from the tristate area of Illinois, Iowa, and Wisconsin. Shagbark had catered to overnight guests only from mid-November through March, but the chair lift and dining room had been open year-round and the grounds were always available, on request, for group outings.

The inn had been an essential part of Shannon's childhood, for she'd come to live with Agatha after her parents were killed in a boating accident when she was only four years old, but she could no longer envision Shagbark as it had appeared in its heyday. A sense of desolation swept over her as she realized that memories of happier times had been overshadowed by the events of seven years ago; events that had reached their climax on the night of the fire.

Afterward she'd followed her grandmother's advice and severed some of her ties with the past cleanly, even ruthlessly, and doing so had been like amputating the most vital part of herself. It had taken a long time for the wounds to heal. Agatha knew this, and that she had asked Dr. Follensbee to summon her granddaughter home was evidence of how seriously ill she must be.

With one trembling hand Shannon absently pushed a silky strand of leaf-brown hair away from her forehead. For all of her misguided efforts to postpone the confrontation with the truth, nothing was changed. *Agatha MacLeod was dying.* Dr. Follensbee had said as much during their telephone conversation.

"We diagnosed the malignancy over a year ago," he'd disclosed, "but Agatha didn't want to worry you until it became absolutely necessary that you be informed. I ordered another scan last week, and it looks as if that time has come."

"Does Grandmother know you're telling me?"

"Yes. As a matter of fact, she asked me to. She specifically asked me to say that she's sorry she couldn't tell you herself, but she hasn't reached the point where she can rely on being able to talk about it with any degree of objectivity."

Shannon's hands had suddenly become so unsteady that

she could barely hold on to the receiver. "Is my grandmother in pain?"

"So far we've been able to keep her fairly comfortable," the doctor had replied.

So far. Shannon had been assailed by the implications of that qualification, and she'd silently entreated, "Please, God, Gran's already had more than her share of suffering. Don't add to it."

Finally, dreading the answer the doctor might give, she'd forced herself to inquire, "How long does Gran have?"

"It's hard to say." For a few moments George Follensbee was silent. Agatha MacLeod had been one of the patients he'd inherited when he'd taken over his father's practice. Over the years he had come to look upon her as a friend, but when he continued speaking, he succeeded in masking his personal grief with a professional demeanor. "I'm sorry, Shannon, but it could be a matter of weeks. At most—perhaps three months."

That her grandmother's time was so limited lent an urgency to Shannon's movements as she shifted into first gear and guided the Volkswagen back into the roadway. When a narrower lane branched away from the drive that led to the inn, she followed this track through a dense stand of oak trees.

"Only three months," she reminded herself, and already four days of that was gone!

After several hundred yards the oaks thinned and the multiangular sprawl of a house could be seen. Against the gentler hues of the woods that surrounded it, the russet-colored cedar of its siding seemed discordant and out of place. It rambled over several levels in order to accommodate to the knoll on which it stood, and because there were

14

no windows in its northern façade, Shannon thought it resembled random-sized boxes tumbling down the hillside, but the dwelling came as no surprise to her.

For as long as she could recall, her Uncle Dennis had threatened to replace the original farmhouse, and when she'd heard that Dennis had used some of the money from the insurance settlement to carry out that threat, she had expected the new house to reflect his avant-garde tastes rather than Agatha's preference for bric-a-brac.

Another car was parked near the double front doors, and as she pulled in behind the gleaming Mercedes she was relieved to see that the huge old hickory trees that shaded the driveway still flourished. Of everything she had seen of her childhood home, they alone were unchanged and blessedly familiar.

The hickories had provided welcome coolness in the summer and shelter from winter's icy gales. In the fall they'd offered mounds of bright-colored leaves to romp in and a generous bounty of delicious thin-shelled nuts that she and her friends had harvested and roasted in the fireplace at the lodge.

More than once Shannon remembered her grandmother telling her, "I'm like these old trees—tough and homely and resilient."

"Tough and resilient, I'll go along with. But homely?" Shannon would counter, shaking her head. "Not you, Gran. You're one of the most beautiful ladies I know."

It was true that Agatha was one of those rare women whose personality made her seem more and more attractive as one became better acquainted with her. But as an adolescent Agatha O'Brien had been an ugly duckling, and even when she had belatedly blossomed into something of a swan, she persisted in seeing herself as awkward, rawboned, and plain.

To compensate for this, she concentrated on cultivating a lively wit, her own brand of charm, and, above all else, an uncompromising sense of fair play. She'd never fully appreciated how unique this combination was, and she never stopped marveling that Gavin MacLeod, one of the most eligible men in Jo Daviess County, had fallen in love with her, married her, and made her the mother of two handsome sons.

She'd made no secret of her grief when Murray, who was the younger of the boys, died. But if she'd ever had any regrets that Dennis's character did not live up to the promise of his powerful physique and clean-cut profile, she kept them to herself.

Agatha regarded the subdued loveliness of her grand-daughter as nothing less than miraculous. Just to see Shannon's winsome smile made her want to pinch herself to make sure she hadn't imagined it all. Moreover, she admired the strong core of determination underlying Shannon's delicate appearance. Dennis might consider Shannon's sensitivity to be a sign of weakness, but Agatha knew that the girl's capacity for tenderness arose from strength. It reminded her of her beloved Gavin and endeared her granddaughter to her all the more.

For these reasons, and because Shannon was all she had left of Murray, it was no wonder that she indulged the girl a bit. Dennis accused his mother of *overindulging* Shannon. He warned Agatha that Shannon would come to expect everyone to treat her with such loving deference. He cautioned that Shannon would feel such privileged treatment was owed her by some kind of natural right, but Agatha discounted his advice.

She knew that Dennis resented his niece. He was jealous of Shannon, just as he'd been jealous of Murray, and Agatha blamed herself for this. She felt that, with her inability to convince Dennis that she'd loved both of her boys equally, she'd failed her eldest son.

She wanted so badly to demonstrate to Dennis that she loved him and had confidence in his judgment, that she'd handed responsibility for the management of the inn over to him. And because she couldn't bear to acknowledge her suspicions that Dennis was misusing his authority, seven years ago Agatha had supported her son in opposing the romance between Shannon and Adam Byrne.

Her first inclination was to try to make light of the affair, to encourage Shannon to see it in what she considered its proper perspective.

"It's to be expected that a teen-aged girl will have her fair share of crushes," Agatha had insisted. "And that's *all* it is, Shannon—a crush."

Shannon had proved to be surprisingly adamant. "Did *you*, Gran?" she'd argued. "Did you have crushes?"

"That's neither here nor there," Agatha quickly evaded. "The point is that you're attaching far more importance to your feelings for Adam than they deserve, simply because you've waited so long. You're eighteen years old, and he's the first young man you've shown any interest in, except as a pal. Heavens! Your friend Meredith Erskine has been falling in and out of love at least once a week since she was twelve!"

"I'm not Merry," Shannon protested stiffly.

"I know that, and I thank God for it every day. I'm not sure I could survive trying to raise a little minx like her. But on this subject I'd place much more credence in Mer-

17

ry's opinion than yours. Lord knows she's had enough experience to be a qualified expert."

"What if Adam and I agree to wait—"

"That would make no difference. Adam Byrne is the worst sort of scoundrel. He's been given every opportunity to prove himself, yet for all his privileged background he's done nothing but wander irresponsibly all over the world and break his poor father's heart. He's his mother all over again."

Ignoring the impulse to question the sincerity of Agatha's uncharacteristic display of concern for Edwin Byrne, Shannon replied heatedly, "You've obviously been listening to Uncle Dennis! Adam is *not* a scoundrel, and I'd hardly call working for two years with an oceanographic project irresponsible wandering."

Her granddaughter's tone was so impassioned that Agatha felt herself wavering.

"Oh, Gran," Shannon softly exclaimed, "I love Adam so much! If only you'd spend some time with him; give him a chance—"

"Never! Adam is not worthy of you and nothing will ever change that."

To shore up her weakening convictions, Agatha had spoken more strongly than she'd intended to, and Shannon's expression was stricken. Seeing this, she softened her approach. "Can't you understand, love, that you're in way over your head. The most that Adam Byrne will ever give you is a few memories to warm your bed on winter nights. You deserve so much more than that."

If anyone said such a thing to her now, Shannon thought, she'd have the definitive comeback. "There are no guarantees," she'd say blithely, "that anyone will get what they deserve. And for that small favor, I say, 'Amen'!"

Her eyes might still be the same violet-shadowed gray, but she was no longer blinded by the stars in them. They had all been washed away by her eighteen-year-old's tears. Now, at twenty-five, her glance was more measuring than dreamy.

As she got out of the car she told herself, "The secret is to expect *nothing* from anyone. At least that way one is never disappointed."

No sooner had this thought surfaced than Shannon was gripped by a feeling of disgust that she had resorted to such easy cynicism. Her self-contempt stung her into action, and without further delay she pulled her luggage out of the Volkswagen and purposefully set off down the walk toward the house.

She was wrestling with the heavy suitcases, clumsily juggling them about in her attempt to free one hand so that she could ring the bell, when the front door was thrown open. The suddenness of its opening startled her, and she was stunned when she recognized the dark-haired man whose lean, wide-shouldered frame filled the doorway.

Wordlessly Shannon stared up at the man. Surely her mind must be playing tricks on her. Adam Byrne couldn't possibly be *here,* in her uncle's house. She must be imagining that he was because he'd dominated her thoughts during the final hours of her journey.

The man reached out to take the cases from her, and she closed her eyes momentarily, as if to dispel an apparition, but when she opened them, she still saw Adam's rough-hewn features.

"Hello, Shannon," he said easily.

She moistened her dry lips. It wasn't fair that after all this time she should still feel the same instantaneous attraction to him.

"What are you doing here?" The question was tinged with unexpected truculence, and as she followed Adam into the dimly lighted foyer, exerting herself to project a friendlier note, she said, "This *is* a surprise."

"And not a pleasant one," Adam hazarded coolly.

"You've forgotten," she replied stiltedly, "I've learned not to care for surprises, pleasant or otherwise."

"You're right," Adam agreed with courteous indifference, "I had forgotten."

Instead of putting her cases down as she'd thought he would, he led the way along the hall, silently guiding her up a shallow flight of stairs and into what was apparently a bedroom wing.

Adam was obviously well acquainted with the house, and Shannon found it bewildering that he should be so at home in her uncle's domain. She formed only a hazy impression of ankle-deep carpets blending endlessly into an expanse of linen-covered walls. Here and there the monotone of pale oyster was relieved by one or another of the abstract paintings from Dennis's collection. They ranged the length of the hall like bold pools of primary brilliance in an otherwise colorless sea.

When they neared the end of the corridor, Adam stepped to one side and motioned to her to precede him into one of the bedrooms.

"Your grandmother thought you'd prefer this room," he explained as he stacked her luggage on the rack at the foot of the bed. "It's in the same relative location as your old bedroom."

Shannon crossed to the windows and looked out toward

20

the willow thicket on the far side of the garden. She could just make out the intricate tracery of wrought iron that decorated the roof of the gazebo.

"The view is the same," she murmured. Her spirits lifted at this proof that her uncle's dislike for the past had not yet extended to the demolition of the summerhouse.

"Impedimenta" was Dennis's disdainful way of referring to any family memento, but in Shannon's opinion he did not admire progress nearly as much as he abhorred reminders of his father.

Gavin MacLeod had come very close to being a Renaissance man, and Dennis's Achilles' heel was that he'd felt obliged to live in his father's shadow. Whatever Gavin tried his hand at had turned to pure gold. He'd earned some fame as a sportsman, and he'd had an unimpeachable reputation as a business and community leader. He'd been valued as a friend and looked up to as a churchman and family man. A classical scholar, he'd read the *Iliad* in Greek. He'd sung tenor with the choral society, played viola in a string quartet, and won prizes at the county fair with his watercolors and roses and gamehens.

Dennis, on the other hand, had been born under an unlucky star. He'd always been in competition with Gavin, never realizing that since he was the sole entrant, it was a competition he couldn't possibly win.

While Shannon was contemplating all this, Adam was busy with his own thoughts.

The sunlight coming in the window played through Shannon's hair, weaving a tawny aureole from the errant tendrils that had escaped the prim coil at the nape of her neck. Seeing her this way, Adam remembered that she'd worn her hair loose before. He remembered that her hair was fine and straight and soft to touch. His memory was so vivid that he could feel its silky texture between his fingers.

She'd once told him that when she was a little girl, she'd been a "true blonde," but as she grew up her hair had gradually darkened until, when she applied for her first driver's license, she'd listed her hair color as "brown."

Agatha described it more accurately, calling it "topaz." As for him, he'd always thought it was the color of wild honey. He still did.

When Shannon turned to face Adam, he was leaning against the doorjamb. His arms were folded across his chest, and he was making no attempt to disguise his speculative interest in her.

"Do I pass muster?" she asked tartly.

Adam smiled. "Do you want an honest answer?"

As if his opinion of her didn't matter in the least, she said jauntily, "Why not?"

"You look tired, you're too thin, and I prefer your hair down, but you'll do."

"Such lavish praise!" she exclaimed. "Aren't you afraid it will go to my head?"

Adam's grin broadened, and she studied him as openly as he was studying her. For the first time she noticed the silvery glints in the dark hair at his temples. The parenthetic lines that ran from his nostrils to the corners of his mouth were more deeply scored, and new lines fanned outward from his eyes. He was thinner, too; or perhaps this was an illusion created by the finely pinstriped fabric of his suit. But for all this the years had not been unkind to him.

Adam had once commented that a person *earned* the face they had at thirty-five. He was only thirty-three, but if his theory were correct, one could draw the conclusion that he'd led a fascinating life, because "fascinating" was the word that best described him.

He'd never been handsome in the accepted definition of the term. With his high cheekbones, deepset eyes, and craggy jaw, his features were too irregular for that. But his attraction for the opposite sex was far more potent than mere good looks could confer.

He was the most self-contained, ruggedly independent man Shannon had ever known—and the most disturbing. His personal dynamism and his air of self-assurance were overwhelming. Where women were concerned he was damnably knowing and, at the same time, lustily male!

Hastily, in an effort to rein in her truant thoughts, Shannon inquired, "How is my grandmother?"

"She's feeling a bit rocky today. They've started her on a new course of chemotherapy, and the side effects can be grim."

"If they've begun giving her a new drug," Shannon eagerly postulated, "that must mean there's still a chance she'll respond!"

"Dr. Follensbee doesn't think so," Adam declared flatly. "He told us that he doesn't want to raise any false hopes. This therapy is experimental, and he's started Agatha on it mainly to assure that she'll keep fighting."

The glow of optimism faded from Shannon's eyes, and he continued in a gentler tone. "Agatha is resting just now. Since everyone else had gone out, she asked me to stick around in case you arrived." He flicked back his shirt cuff and glanced at his wristwatch. "She'll probably sleep for another hour or so."

Shannon's throat worked as she choked back a rush of tears, but this was the only outward sign of her emotions. Seven years ago she would have run to Adam and cried out her disappointment in the warm haven of his arms. Now she knew that there were no "safe" places. She knew that Adam would never again offer her that refuge, even if she wanted him to.

"What *are* you doing here, Adam?"

"You haven't heard?" He quirked one eyebrow at her, expressing his disbelief. The mannerism was very familiar and at one time had been so terribly dear that, as if it were a conditioned reflex, Shannon's pulses quickened.

"I'm Agatha's attorney," he said, "and, I'd like to believe, her friend. I've been her legal and business adviser since Gil and I opened our office in Galena three years ago."

Shannon's eyes widened with astonishment. "How did Gran happen to come to you?"

Adam shrugged. "I think it would be best if you asked your grandmother that question."

"What does Dennis think about this arrangement?"

"It's out of his hands, so there's nothing he can do about it, much as he might like to." He paused briefly. "It might be more to the point if I asked about your reaction. What do you think of it?"

"I—I'm pleased." Shannon was dismayed that she had stammered her response. "I always thought you'd be an excellent lawyer," she went on more firmly, "and I never doubted your integrity."

"We both know you had no reason to," Adam countered smoothly.

Shannon had no defense against this charge, for it was the truth, and a change of subject seemed advisable. "Where is Uncle Dennis?" she asked.

Adam's eyebrows shot up expressively. "You have been

out of touch, haven't you! Hasn't your grandmother told you that Dennis has joined the ranks of the gainfully employed?"

"No." She made no effort to conceal the fact that she was taken aback by this news. "Where is he working?"

"At Eagles Nest."

"Eagles Nest!" Shannon echoed faintly. That explained Agatha's failure to keep her informed. During the past seven years both of them had religiously avoided any mention of Adam, and because he'd temporarily assumed control of the Byrne family holdings after his father's heart attack, this ban had covered happenings at Eagles Nest as well. "But why—"

"Your uncle hadn't much choice," Adam replied. "He needed a job. He ran through the insurance money building this place, and he still refuses to sell Shagbark acreage to the Byrnes. Since Eagles Nest is the only purchaser that's likely to pay what he's asking, he hasn't been able to find another buyer."

Shannon shook her head in confusion. "I can't believe I'm hearing this!" she exclaimed. "Even if Uncle Dennis was willing to work for you, why did you agree to hire him?"

"Dennis is not entirely lacking in marketable skills. He's our social director and he's quite the glad-hander. The middle-aged women love him and their husbands tell me that he's a real 'card.' Besides," Adam pointed out crisply, "I thought it advisable to arrange things so I could keep an eye on him. He has no access to the books or to large sums of cash, so I don't have to worry about him ripping us off or stabbing me in the back!"

"You don't pull any punches, do you?" She lifted her

chin, proudly withstanding the inner pain he'd inflicted with his bluntness.

Without responding to her feeble protest, Adam pushed lithely away from the door and came toward her. It was not until she felt the shock of his touch that she realized how badly she'd wanted him to touch her, and she fixed her gaze on his shirt collar. She was suffocatingly aware of him, intoxicated by his nearness, as he took her hand between both of his and opened the tense clutch of her fist.

"No rings," he observed softly as he straightened her slender fingers. "Does that mean you're not seriously involved with anyone just now?"

Damning her inability to pull away from him, Shannon weakly shook her head. "No—er, yes!" She drew in a deep, steadying breath. "What I mean is, no, I'm not—involved."

"You've never wanted to marry again?"

"No." This time her response was delivered in a tremulous whisper. "And you?"

"No." He hadn't raised his voice, but his tone was firmly vehement, as if he considered marriage to be a sentence for some sort of capital offense.

She might have imagined the tightening of his hold on her hand. It was brief enough that it was barely perceptible, but all the same it compelled her to meet his eyes. They were brutally assessing, and their obsidian depths were so cold that she was immediately sobered by them. In the same instant that she sought release, Adam let go of her hand.

"No doubt you'd like to be alone for a while, to unpack your things or whatever it is women do after a long drive," he suggested with curious abruptness. "I'll wait for you in the living room."

"No! I—Would you show me where my grandmother's room is? If it's all right, I'd like to sit with her until she wakes up."

CHAPTER TWO

In the days immediately following Shannon's return Agatha's condition underwent a marked improvement. Within a week she felt well enough to spend most of the day out of bed. The troublesome nausea had vanished, and her appetite was restored. She regained her usual optimism as well.

She seemed so much better that Alice and Ned Penrose, the couple who had been housekeeper and gardener-handyman to the MacLeod household for so many years that they were like part of the family, conjectured that the new medication Dr. Follensbee had prescribed was responsible for the change. Shannon and Dennis were more than willing to go along with this encouraging point of view.

Much as he hated to, the doctor had to disabuse them of this notion when additional tests revealed the ineffectiveness of the drug. There had been no remission.

He made a special trip to the hospital in Dubuque, where he met with Agatha's son and granddaughter. There, in the flickering semidarkness of the reading room in the Radiology Department, surrounded by Agatha's X rays, which were affixed to the viewing screens that lined the walls, he offered Shannon and her uncle the only consolation he could.

"Be grateful that she's not suffering," he said. "Be grateful that she's able to enjoy this respite. Make the most of it. She could start going downhill any day."

Confronted with the images that attested to the rapid growth of the metastases and their invasion of once healthy tissue—into lung, into bone—Shannon and Dennis were convinced. Even a layman could see the awful extent of the lesions, and it was impossible to ignore the evidence they had seen with their own eyes.

They left the hospital and began the half-hour drive back to Galena, subdued and profoundly saddened by what they'd seen.

"I've never felt so damned helpless in all my life," Dennis plaintively cried as he drove eastward over the bridge that spanned the Mississippi. He made no attempt to hide the tears that welled into his eyes. "There's *nothing* we can do, is there?"

Shannon could gauge his hopelessness by the somber note in his voice, and she suggested huskily, "We can do what Dr. Follensbee advised. We can make the most of each day Gran has left."

Shaking his head disparagingly, Dennis lamented, "That seems so futile—so paltry!"

"We'll have to make it be enough."

After they had traveled a few miles in silence, Shannon softly disclosed, "I know how you feel, Uncle Dennis. I feel the same way."

Her uncle darted a calculating look at her. "Yes," he slowly acceded, "I believe you do."

"If you ever want to let your hair down, I'll be available. And there are Alice and Ned. They love Gran too."

In a rare display of affection, Dennis reached over to pat Shannon's hand, saying, "Thank you, my dear, for reminding me I'm not entirely alone."

Both of them were comforted by their renewed sense of kinship. Since her return an uneasy truce had existed between them, but Dennis had been pleasant to Shannon primarily out of gratitude for the palliative effect she'd had on his mother's condition. Only now did he begin to appreciate the fact that Shannon was *family*.

"Have you forgiven me for what happened seven years ago?" he asked. All at once it seemed imperative to him that she should have.

Shannon was moved by her uncle's appeal, but in spite of his earnestness she couldn't honestly say she'd forgiven him. The lies he'd told had cost her so much that it was possible she'd never be able to absolve him. And he'd never actually said he was sorry for what he'd done. He still hadn't admitted to any wrongdoing.

"I understand why you did the things you did," she said gently, and though her answer was evasive, Dennis seemed to find it satisfactory.

Later that day Agatha asked much the same thing of Shannon. As a surprise for her grandmother Shannon had given the gazebo a thorough cleaning. She'd found the old wicker furniture in the basement of the house, and before she and Ned had carried it outdoors, she'd laundered the slipcovers for the seat cushions. The paisley print of the heavy cretonne was badly faded, the reds reduced almost to pink, the onetime blues turned gray, but the old slipcovers would have to do until she could make some new ones. She had even given the wrought-iron railing of the summerhouse a bright coat of paint.

When Agatha woke from her nap that afternoon, Shanon helped her walk down the recently cleared pathway through the willows.

Her grandmother's frailty was a painful reminder of Dr. Follensbee's prognosis, for she leaned heavily on Shannon's arm as they strolled through trees. Agatha's once vigorous step was palsied, and her hand on Shannon's arm was so wasted that it was very nearly transparent.

Just when Shannon began to worry that the distance might be too taxing for her grandmother, they arrived at the edge of the bluff and entered the little clearing that was the site of the gazebo.

"Why, Shannon!" Agatha exclaimed delightedly when she saw the transformation. "It's just like it used to be!"

"It will be, once I've finished sewing some cushion covers. I thought you might like to help me decide which material to order."

Shannon settled Agatha in the chair that had always been her favorite and tucked a lap robe snugly about her legs before she retrieved the swatches of fabric she'd left on the Victorian gossip bench. When she glanced back at her grandmother, she was disconcerted by the vigilance with which Agatha was watching her.

"At the rate you sew," Agatha said firmly, "unless you let me help with them, I'm not going to be around long enough to see them finished."

Tears stung Shannon's eyes and she hurriedly averted them. The colorful floral pattern on the scrap of polished cotton she was holding blurred and ran together as the tears spilled through her lashes.

"I'm sorry to be so blunt," Agatha went on, "but we both know that I'm dying, and I'm tired of everyone avoiding the subject. I find that I can't face the prospect of death alone."

31

"Do you want to talk about it, Gran?" Shannon's voice was low and tormented.

"Not just now." Agatha sounded relieved. "During the day I manage very well. In fact, mostly I feel as if I'm a displaced person and the idea of dying isn't all that unpleasant. So many of my contemporaries have died, and I've lost my husband and my youngest son. There are only a few people who call me by my given name, and I can't remember the last time anyone called me 'Aggie.' I think I miss that more than anything else!"

"Oh, Gran!" Shannon dropped to her knees beside her grandmother. "I can't bear the thought of losing you!"

Tenderly Agatha smoothed the fine wisps of hair away from Shannon's forehead. "Does that mean you've forgiven me for my failure to offer you my support seven years ago?"

"There's nothing to forgive! You only did what you thought best for me."

Agatha's lips thinned to a stern line, and her expression became distant. She stared vacantly at some point in space above Shannon's head, as though she were peering into the past.

"That was the third biggest mistake I ever made," she said, picking up the train of her thoughts as if Shannon hadn't spoken. "My second was allowing Dennis to manage the inn, and my first—well," she added abstractedly, "we won't go into that just now. But my old lady's fears are no excuse. No matter how concerned I was that Adam would only hurt you, I should never have interfered. I should have been willing to let you go. I should have let you live your own life, make your own errors, go after the things that would have made you happy."

Her hand stopped its stroking to rest on Shannon's head

and press it fondly against her blanket-covered knee. "You were so happy that summer," Agatha murmured. "I'd never seen you so happy. You were always laughing. I haven't heard you laugh that way since you've been home." She sighed. "There are times when I miss that happy young woman."

"There are times when I miss her too," Shannon shakily admitted.

"Maybe it's not too late to make amends."

Shannon's head jerked upright. "What do you mean?" she asked in an anguished whisper. "You're not counting on a reconciliation between Adam and me, are you? Oh God, Gran! Is that why you've become so friendly with him?"

"Don't be silly! It's just that when I meet my maker I don't want it on my conscience that I did nothing to resolve the preposterous feud between the MacLeods and the Byrnes."

Agatha was the very image of injured innocence. Her protest was mild, shaded with the proper amount of exasperation to make it seem genuine. "I don't know what you're getting at, Shannon! Adam is my lawyer. He's handled a number of business transactions for me, and his partner, Gil Rutherford, made out my will. Over the past three years I've come to know and respect Adam as a man, as well as my attorney. It's only natural that I should see him now and again."

"Now and again!" Shannon shook her head incredulously as she repeated her grandmother's phrase. "How can you say that when he's here several times a week? Please, Gran, don't do anything foolish. Adam and I are ancient history. It's useless to try and rewrite events that are best forgotten; to try to rearrange them into a happy ending."

"Shannon, please believe me when I say I've learned my lesson. I wouldn't dream of doing such a thing!" The reassurance was so readily given that Shannon believed her grandmother. She couldn't detect that Agatha had surreptitiously crossed her fingers under the cover of the lap robe.

Agatha had always been proud of her ability to bluff her way out of sticky situations. It was a useful tool, particularly in business dealings. But lying was repugnant to her. She had lied once before, and she'd seen the terrible consequences of her lies. She'd paid dearly, but so had others, and because she held herself accountable for their suffering there were times when her burden of guilt was intolerable. Yet she accepted it as a means of expiation for having been a meddlesome old woman.

From Shannon's horrified reaction Agatha knew it was too early to reveal the truth to her, but her conscience troubled her nonetheless. She swore to herself that soon, very soon, she would tell Shannon the complete story.

As she flexed her cramped fingers Agatha sent up a silent petition for forgiveness. She'd told only white lies, after all, and even those were prompted by the most unselfish intentions. Surely God would not hold them against her.

After dinner that night Shannon revisited the gazebo. She needed a quiet time alone to regroup her defenses, and the gazebo had always been her favorite place for solitude.

Growing up as she had, spending most of her time at the inn, where it was inevitable that there would be crowds of people about, she had soon learned what a precious

34

commodity privacy was. Sometimes, when the pressures became too great, she'd come to the one spot where her privacy was sacrosanct. Even Dennis had never intruded when he'd known she was alone in the summerhouse.

The evening was cool, for it was the second week in September and the sun had disappeared beyond the Mississippi. Only a faint luminescence on the western horizon marked its passing.

The view of the Mississippi was one of the things she liked best about the gazebo. In the pale afterglow of dusk the river's broad channel was nearly indiscernible, with only the running lights of a passing houseboat to define the navigable portion of the waterway.

When she was a little girl, she'd waited in this very spot for the *Delta Queen* to go by. She'd listened for the warning blast of its whistle as it approached the busier stretch of the river near Dubuque, and every time she'd heard the whistle's deep-voiced wail, she had vowed that someday she would book passage on the stern-wheeler.

How magical the riverboats had seemed in those growing-up years when so many things offered enchantment that every day was Christmas and the Fourth of July rolled into one! In those days even the arrival of Chauncey Buxton, the mailman, was exciting, for she'd often spent all of her allowance to send away for the latest "secret decoder ring" or some other treasure that was touted on the cereal packages at the inn. She'd also been an avid collector of boxtops, candy wrappers, tinfoil, and every conceivable type of "gift coupon," and she'd entered so many contests that Chauncey had jokingly accused her of contributing to his sciatica.

"The pain's something fierce today, Miz MacLeod," he'd tell Agatha whenever she inquired as to his health.

"Old Doc Follensbee tells me it's caused by a new disease called 'Shannonitis.' "

Chauncey's teasing hadn't discouraged her, though. She'd continued sending in her entries. For her diligence she'd received a few minor prizes and countless free samples of off-brand products neither she nor anyone she knew would ever buy, along with a miscellaneous assortment of junk mail.

For years she'd occupied herself in this way. Undaunted by her failure to win anything of value, she'd eagerly awaited the delivery of the mail, for who could say what wonders Chauncey might be carrying in his pouch on any given day.

This was how she'd learned that the real reward lay in the *possibility* of winning. She'd realized early on that if she ever received some fabulous prize, she wouldn't find that nearly as satisfying as the promise of success.

In an infinitely more painful way her experience with Adam had reinforced the lesson that the attainment of one's objective could never measure up to the dream of doing so.

She'd fallen in love with Adam Byrne the first time she'd met him. By then, of course, she was older; well past the stage of entering contests.

They had met on an evening very similar to this one. It had been early June, so the chill in the air was unseasonable, but there had been a ripe pumpkin of a moon hanging low in the sky on that night too; a moon so big and round that it seemed artificial. She'd even been sitting in the same chair, but she'd lighted the lamps because she was supposed to be studying for final exams.

Now Shannon sat in the dark, but she looked at the moon, and she remembered.

CHAPTER THREE

In a community as small as Galena, where the population was so stable that half the town was related to the other half, the fact that Shannon MacLeod did not meet Adam Byrne until she was fifteen was unique. It was especially remarkable when one took into account that they were neighbors and that both of their families operated ski lodges.

This unusual set of circumstances was explained by a feud that had had its beginnings more than a hundred years before either Adam or Shannon was born.

It started after the untimely death of Noah Byrne, when a disagreement arose as to who held legal title to the then worthless bluffs beside the river. This boundary dispute had quickly escalated into open warfare when the Byrnes made the unpleasant accusation that the carriage accident in which Noah had lost his life might not have been an accident at all.

Through succeeding generations the aversion of the MacLeods for the Byrnes, and vice versa, was handed down like a birthright, from father to son. Even the gentle Gavin had been caught up in it. Whenever tempers cooled sufficiently that it seemed an armistice might be declared, something happened that incited a new outbreak of hostility between the two families.

Dennis MacLeod's antipathy to the Byrnes dated from the time when he and Edwin Byrne were rivals for the affections of the same young woman.

When Nicole DeCourcey chose Edwin over him, she admitted to Dennis that she'd given in to family pressures. That the Byrnes and the DeCourceys were socially top-drawer was so widely conceded, it had become a standing joke that even their servants had unlisted telephone numbers, and she told Dennis her parents were opposed to a match with him because his people were not from the same lofty echelon of Galena society. Dennis did not take kindly to being relegated to the ranks of the socially inferior.

As it turned out, Nicole was incapable of being faithful to any one man for more than a few months at a time, and her marriage to Edwin was far from happy, but this did nothing to diminish Dennis's antagonism. When Nicole abandoned her husband and son to run away with an out-of-work actor who'd stayed at Eagles Nest one winter, Dennis derived bitter satisfaction from Edwin's loss.

As a youth Dennis had developed the habit of blaming his misfortunes on someone else, and now this tendency became more deeply entrenched than ever. The only difference was that now whatever evil befell him, he laid responsibility for it at the doorstep of Eagles Nest.

When under his management Shagbark Inn began to suffer financial reverses, it was second nature to Dennis to believe that the Byrnes were the root and branch of his problem. And when Edwin Byrne tendered an offer to purchase the hotly contested acreage that included Shagbark's best ski slopes, Dennis's fury reached its zenith.

It was Adam who acted as go-between. He happened to be home that June for the first time since he'd finished college. He'd spent the previous year bumming around Europe, doing some skiing, a good deal of sailing, and honing his talent for photography. This sabbatical had paid off handsomely, for his skills with a camera had enabled him to land an assignment as marine photographer for an oceanographic study that was being funded by the Jaeger Institute. He was looking forward to leaving Galena for Baja California at the end of the month.

Adam had inherited Nicole's wanderlust, and it was partly to soothe his father's hurt feelings that he'd volunteered to act as intermediary between Edwin and Dennis. It was a sore point with Edwin that he showed no inclination to return to Eagles Nest permanently, but he wasn't ready to settle down yet.

Perhaps it was just as well that Dennis was away from home on the evening Adam chose to stop in and collect the formal reply to his father's offer. Her uncle was so incensed over the situation, Shannon wasn't sure what he might have done if he'd been there to witness one of the Byrnes daring to trespass on MacLeod land.

As it was, Agatha and Dennis were away on a buying trip to Chicago, and Alice and Ned Penrose had gone to a revival meeting, so Shannon was the only one at home that night.

She'd gone out to the gazebo to study for an English test, but she'd gotten sidetracked reading *Romeo and Juliet*. She'd done some daydreaming and a lot of weeping over the plight of the star-crossed lovers, and still wrapped in the romance and tragedy of the drama, she'd fallen asleep and dreamed some more. For a very long time after

39

Adam awakened her, she'd thought she must still be dreaming.

He'd seemed the very substance of her dreams. Even at twenty-three, with his rugged hard-muscled body and bold gypsy-dark eyes, he'd had the untamed look of an adventurer. She'd stared at him to the point of rudeness. Her perceptions were heightened by unfamiliar emotions, and she could still recall the smallest detail about the way he was dressed, the things they'd said, the way he moved. She even recalled that he'd carried some sort of document rolled up in one lean hand and that he'd tapped it restlessly against his thigh while he'd stood looking down at her.

"You must be Shannon MacLeod," he'd said.

She closed her eyes quickly, then opened them wide, surprised to hear her dream speaking to her so realistically.

"I wonder why they named you Shannon," he added thoughtfully. "Anyone with eyes like the sun shining on the heather through a storm cloud should be named Grace or Faith or Patience, or something equally inspirational."

She looked up at him, tongue-tied, and when she didn't respond, he said, "Don't get me wrong, though, I'm glad your eyes are lavender-gray. They suit you. They're all softness and unawakened innocence, like the rest of you."

Her face grew rosy with pleased embarrassment at this disarming compliment, and she continued to stare at Adam, utterly spellbound by him.

When she remained silent, he asked, "May I sit down?"

"Please do," she invited, hoping to make amends for having forgotten her manners.

When Adam turned away to move a chair closer to hers, she hastily tucked her blouse more neatly into the waistband of her skirt. She wished she were wearing something other than the clothes she'd worn to school that day. They did nothing for her and made her look every bit as young as she was.

Completely at ease, Adam slouched into his chair, sitting on the end of his spine with his feet propped on the railing.

"I'm Adam Byrne," he announced.

"I know. That is, I guessed that's who you are."

"Is that why you've been staring at me?" His smile removed the sting from the question. "Are you surprised that I don't have horns and a tail?"

"No!" she exclaimed. "It's just that I wasn't expecting anyone."

He nodded gravely. "I can see why. It takes someone very dedicated or very nosy to hack their way through the brambles to Sleeping Beauty's castle."

Although his comment proved that he considered her a child, the path through the willows *was* terribly overgrown, and she smiled at this bit of whimsy. Adam smiled back at her, and in that moment she'd known that she was irrevocably in love with him. But even while he was smiling, he shifted restlessly in his chair, and she resigned herself to the fact that he would soon be leaving.

"When do you expect your uncle?" he asked.

"N-not till tomorrow," she stammered. If only she were older, more gifted at small talk, more like her friend Merry, she might be able to hold his interest. She might be able to detain him, if only for a little while longer. "Could I give him some message?"

"I'd appreciate it if you'd tell him I stopped by."

"Did you want to see him about the ski slopes?"

"Yes," Adam replied. "Since Rainbow Ridge opened, it's been fairly obvious that either Eagles Nest or Shagbark can survive, but not both of them. Not as separate entities, at any rate. Dad hoped that if your uncle isn't interested in selling, he'd agree to meet and discuss the possibility of a merger."

Shannon knew that Dennis was so desperate to recoup his business losses that he'd been gambling more and more heavily. But she also knew how unlikely it was that he would go along with Adam's suggestion.

"I doubt he'll do that," she said.

"It's because of the feud, isn't it?"

When Shannon nodded, confirming this assumption, Adam got to his feet and stalked impatiently around the full circumference of the gazebo. For countless minutes he paced and, as a further safety valve for his temper, he tapped the rolled-up paper against his thigh. At last he stopped pacing and muttered, "It's so damned senseless! I won't deny that my mother can be quite a siren. She certainly has the notches on the bedpost to prove it. But *no woman* is worth carrying a torch or a grudge over for twenty-five minutes, let alone twenty-five years!"

He looked sharply at Shannon, as if he expected her to argue the point. When she didn't, his glance softened and he said, "I suppose it's up to the two of us to put an end to the vendetta between the Byrnes and the MacLeods."

Adam stayed only a few minutes longer that night, and Shannon didn't see him again until after her graduation from high school more than two years later.

She was working full time for her uncle that summer, floating from the clerical staff to the dining room to the housekeeping department, filling in for regular employees who were on vacation. As Adam had predicted, the inn's financial position was steadily worsening. Her uncle had been forced to borrow to the limit the local bank would allow, but he was more opposed than ever to a sale or a merger.

To help with her expenses when she went away to college in the fall, she was saving most of her salary, but when the theater in Galena sponsored a film festival of Humphrey Bogart movies, she couldn't resist subscribing to the series.

None of her friends were interested in going, so she went on her own. It was on the Wednesday they featured *Casablanca* and *To Have and Have Not* that she met Adam for the second time.

Shannon was so engrossed in the movie that she didn't notice when a late arrival slid into the seat next to hers. Her eyes were glued to the screen, the box of buttered popcorn she held in one hand forgotten. With her free hand she furtively wiped away tears when Dooley Wilson as Sam played "As Time Goes By"; when Rick, the tough-vulnerable Bogart character, toasted the woman he'd loved and lost; when Ingrid Bergman as Ilsa opted for the coolly cerebral Laszlo and boarded the plane, leaving Rick to walk away into the fog.

If anything, her tears became more copious at the final fadeout. The credits started to roll, but she was unaware that the man next to her was offering her a handkerchief until he waved it right under her nose.

Startled out of her involvement with the characters on the screen, Shannon stared blankly at the man. His craggy features were familiar, but she was confused by his beard.

Leaning close, he whispered, "I'll trade the use of this for some of that popcorn."

In the next moment the house lights came on and she recognized Adam.

"It's you!" she gasped.

"Is it a deal?" Adam asked.

"All right," she agreed faintly, handing him the box when his suggestive glance at the popcorn prompted her to exchange it for the handkerchief.

"I see you're still devoted to crying over unhappy love affairs," he remarked. "Wasn't it *Romeo and Juliet* the last time we met?"

Shannon took her time drying her tears, holding the handkerchief in front of her face longer than was strictly necessary in order to hide the vivid color in her cheeks.

"You're very observant," she said uneasily.

Adam shrugged. "It's a result of working as a photographer."

"Is that what you've been doing?"

He nodded, tossed another handful of popcorn into his mouth, and chewed in thoughtful silence.

"I've decided that Ansel Adams has nothing to fear from me, though." He grinned wryly. "That's why I'm going to law school this fall."

"I'd like to see some of your pictures sometime," Shannon admitted shyly.

"Sure thing," Adam said, pleasantly noncommittal. He was absently rubbing the backs of his fingers against the beard, and when he noticed her watching him he stuck out his chin and asked, "What do you think of it?"

Without stopping to choose her words, she replied, "I think if you had a parrot and a gold earring, you'd make a terrific pirate!"

"Thanks," he said, taking her critique as a compliment. "Does it itch?"

Adam laughed. "No, it's beyond that stage. Frankly, it's more trouble than it's worth to keep the damned thing

44

trimmed now that I'm back in civilization. I've considered shaving it off, but I'm reluctant to go around two-toned for the time it would take the lower half of my face to tan."

Shannon nodded solemnly. Thinking his tan was so dark he must have been outdoors a great deal of the time, she asked where he'd been working for the past two years, and he told her a little about Ballenas Bay, Cabo San Lucas, and the Galapagos Islands. When the lights were dimmed and the second feature began, the woman in front of them turned around to give them a disapproving look, putting an end to their conversation.

Although Shannon kept her eyes fixed on the screen, she saw none of the second feature. She was far too aware of the lithe strength of Adam's body in the seat next to hers to be able to concentrate on anything but him. Because it was the first teaming of Bogart and Bacall, she had seen *To Have and Have Not* at least as many times as she'd seen the rest of Bogart's films combined, and she was knowledgeable enough to discuss it intelligently with Adam when he drove her home.

During the drive Shannon was even more intensely conscious of Adam. She was conscious of the inchoate yearnings of her own body as well. From the corner of her eye she studied Adam's brigand-like profile and longed to run her fingertips over the spare line of his cheek, to trace the well-defined angle of an eyebrow. She longed to know if his skin felt as smooth and warm as it looked.

The beard seemed to draw attention to his wide, mobile mouth. His upper lip was thin and the lower one was full and sensual, and she wondered what it would be like to be kissed by him.

She wished she could elicit more than his friendly interest; wished she could make him see her as more than a fellow Bogart fan.

If she'd had even a tenth of Merry's experience with men, perhaps she'd know how to go about evoking his interest in her as a *woman*. She wished she were fantastically beautiful. Failing that, she wished she could be so scintillatingly bright and clever that Adam would find her unforgettable. But she feared that the impression she was making was negligible rather than indelible. She was afraid it would not even survive the night.

It was sheer desperation that impelled Shannon to behave so recklessly when Adam stopped the car at the front door of her house. Before she could lose her nerve, she turned to him, threw her arms around his neck, and pressed her mouth to his. She felt him tense with surprise, and his hands clamped about her wrists in order to pry her arms away, but she amazed herself with her persistence and clung even closer to him.

Slowly Adam's hands relaxed, relinquishing their bruising grip on her wrists to skim along her arms and settle on her shoulders. His initial reaction of surprise was supplanted by admiration for the insouciance with which Shannon had thumbed her nose at convention, and he assumed command of the kiss.

His lips softened and moved over hers from side to side, with little prying, nibbling motions, and Shannon dared to twine her hands through the crisp dark hair that grew so thickly at his temples, to sample the wiry texture of his beard. When her eager fingers dipped inside the collar of his shirt and found the heavy chain of some sort of medallion, she followed its course until she was diverted by the hard warmth of his chest.

Adam had intended to keep the kiss brief. He'd meant

for it to convey only brotherly affection that would soften the blow of rejection. But Shannon's mouth was incredibly sweet, her young body was pliant and warm, and although her response was inexperienced, it was irresistibly intense. He was dismayed to discover how deeply stirred he was by her. Against his will his hands tightened their hold on her, probing the fine bones of her shoulders and arching her body against his until he could feel the soft imprint of her breasts upon his chest.

He traced the outline of her mouth with the tip of his tongue, and the sudden onrush of desire that buffeted Shannon taught her how to respond. Her lips parted to offer him access to the honeyed recesses of her mouth, and his kiss deepened into one of searing passion.

When Adam finally wrenched his mouth away from hers, he was as shaken as Shannon.

"This is crazy," he muttered raggedly. "You're only a child!"

"I'm seventeen," she countered breathlessly.

"So old?" He sounded amused, but he pulled her close again. His lips trailed across her cheek to brush transient little kisses on her eyelids and in the sensitive hollow beneath her ear. "Then you've probably done this hundreds of times."

"No," she whispered.

"You're a fast learner," he murmured against her mouth. The touch of his lips against hers sent tremors of excitement racing through her.

"Necessity is the mother of invention," she quoted huskily.

Adam raised his head and looked down at her. "Is it?" he asked coolly.

"What?" Shannon wished he would kiss her again.

47

"My kissing you. Is it a necessity?"

"Yes! Oh, yes!" She spoke on a sigh as she pulled his mouth down to hers.

This time his kiss was longer and deeper, but there was no tenderness in it. There was not a hint of love either, nor even affection. And there was no restraint in the way Adam's hands roughly explored the soft contours of her breasts. There was only frank arousal, as if any woman would do.

Shannon knew what he was demonstrating to her in this cruelly disillusioning way, and tears shimmered in her eyes when he finally thrust her away from him.

Adam studied her as she sagged weakly against the car door. Her face was downcast and turned to one side, so that her hair spilled forward, long and silky, partially veiling her tears. For a few moments he permitted his gaze to linger on the delicate curve of her cheek, on the pure ellipse of an eyelid with its fringe of gold-tipped lashes. He saw the trembling innocence of her mouth, the sweet roundness of her breasts, the lissome taper of a thigh. In the sylphlike girl he saw the woman she would become. He saw the rich promise of beauty and passion, and it required monumental self-control not to touch her, but when he spoke, his tone was impersonal.

"You see, Shannon," he said softly, *"That's* necessity. And that's what you can expect when you make a pass at a man who's picked you up."

A hot tide of color washed up the pale stem of her neck, and he laughed harshly. "I believe you when you say you haven't done a lot of petting. From the look of you just now, I'd say you're the kind of young lady who won't be satisfied with anything less than love, marriage, kids, and *permanence.*" He shook his head ruefully. "In fact, you're

48

the kind of old-fashioned girl who strikes terror in the heart of a wary bachelor like myself."

Shannon's eyes flew open, and she stared at Adam in astonishment.

"I'm not ashamed to admit that you frighten me, Shannon MacLeod," he explained. "One look at you, and I want to run for my life!"

"But not from me, Adam." He had succeeded in disconcerting her, but she contradicted him with the coolness of certainty. "It's yourself you want to run from."

While she collected her handbag and slipped its strap over her shoulder, Shannon expected Adam to make some rebuttal. He remained silent, however, and his face was closed and hard. He still hadn't replied when she opened the door and climbed out of the car.

She started down the walk toward the house, but she had gone only a few steps before she turned back to call to him, as if without interruption, "Even if necessity were all you could ever give me, I'd rather have that with you, Adam Byrne, than all those other things without you!"

Shannon saw Adam a few more times that summer. Since he was dating Meredith Erskine's older sister, Pamela, their paths were bound to cross from time to time. He was friendly enough on those occasions, but they were never alone and the most he ever said to her was "hello." Evidently Pamela didn't like his beard, because he got rid of it. Although she envied Pamela, Adam seemed so unattainable that Shannon wasn't truly jealous of the older girl.

Pamela was only twenty-one, but in experience and sophistication she was light years ahead of Shannon. For a while she'd lived in Chicago, where her glorious auburn hair, her elegant, willowy figure, and the graceful sway of her walk had earned her deserved recognition as a model. The previous winter, after a brief marriage had ended in divorce, she'd returned to Galena and opened a boutique in one of the restored buildings on Main Street. Her store had been open for business only a few months, but already Pamela's sense of style and her ability to foresee which of the latest trends in women's apparel would gain acceptance had made her Galena's guru of fashion.

Pamela was striking rather than beautiful, but she was always fastidiously groomed, her manner was regal, and she capitalized on her dramatic coloring so skillfully that she gave the impression of beauty.

There were more than a few similarities between Pamela and Meredith, but there were also some vast differences. For example, no one would ever dream of calling Pamela "Pam." She just wasn't the sort of person with whom one used a diminutive.

Like her sister, Merry was a green-eyed redhead, but she was almost buxom, and her nature was placid rather than high-strung. She studiously avoided the least semblance of Pamela's high gloss. Instead, she affected a vaguely rumpled look. She'd leave a button undone, or her hair would be slightly mussed, or perhaps she'd use a lipstick that was just a shade away from coordinating with the color of the dress she was wearing. Her habitual expression was a heavy-lidded half-smile.

When Pamela accused Merry of looking as if she'd just crawled out of bed, Merry was unoffended.

"That's the general idea," she admitted amiably. "The boys seem to think it's sexy."

"Maybe the 'boys' do," Pamela warned. "But a *man* might be tempted to think you look like a tart!"

"If I find that's the case," Merry drawled, "I'll change my image."

"In the meantime, do me a favor," Pamela haughtily instructed. "Don't tell *anyone* you get most of your clothes from my boutique."

Merry good-naturedly agreed. She knew she lacked Pamela's chic and she might not be glamorous, but she was right about one thing. The boys thought she was sexy.

Shannon admired Merry's and Pamela's self-confidence, and she studied Pamela, trying to determine what it was about her that Adam found most appealing.

"Personally, I can't figure out what Adam Byrne sees in my sister," was Merry's frank comment. "It's probably just that the pickings are so slim hereabouts. But whatever it is, I hope it lasts. Adam must be a wonderful lover. Pamela's become almost human since she's been seeing so much of him."

Shannon was shocked, and it showed. "Surely you don't believe they're having an affair."

"Oh, for Pete's sake, Shannon!" Merry exclaimed disgustedly. "Grow up!"

In the year that followed, Shannon did her utmost to heed that homely advice.

CHAPTER FOUR

By the next June, Shannon had put away the things of childhood. At some time during the fall semester she had arrived at the mistaken notion that maturity consisted of engaging in one or two harmless flirtations, quoting from obscure passages of Descartes, and wearing unrelieved black. Gobs of makeup also helped. By spring she had convinced herself that she was totally adult.

As if to confirm this belief, her figure had suddenly ripened. Her weight redistributed itself so that her waist was smaller, her hips fuller, and she required the next size larger brassiere. Unlike most of her friends, she almost always wore a bra. It wasn't as if she really needed one, but to Shannon this flimsy undergarment was a badge of her newly acquired adult status.

At the beginning of summer vacation she thought that the completion of a year of college automatically made her an authority on any subject.

"I sent my granddaughter off to the University of Minnesota, and they sent me back a stranger," Agatha laughingly told Alice Penrose one morning when Shannon had finished expounding on some especially pedantic topic. "I ask her if she enjoyed the shrimp salad she had for lunch and I get a lecture on ecology. If I ask her 'why,' that's good for a half-hour of 'why not.' "

To Shannon she indulgently complained, "All I did, love, was remark that it's a lovely day, and you bombarded me with a philosophical dissertation on truth and beauty!"

Smiling sheepishly, Shannon asked, "Am I that bad?"

"Not if you can still see the funny side of the way you're behaving," Agatha replied. "As long as you can see the humor in it, there's hope for you!"

"I'll try to, Gran," Shannon promised. "And you're right, you know. It *is* a lovely day."

Every day was lovely that summer. It was a halcyon time that was filled with endless opportunities for enjoyment. Even the weather was perfect. The days were sunny and warm and it rained only at night, but that was enough to keep the countryside green and lush. The climbing roses that grew in profusion in Shagbark's gardens were arrested at the peak of fragrant bloom.

Dennis wasn't nearly as worried about finances that summer. On the contrary, he was optimistic.

At first Shannon couldn't understand this turnabout. From what she'd seen of business since her return home, its steady decline hadn't stopped. Because her uncle's secretary had given notice at the end of May, Shannon was working in the manager's office, so she was in a position to know that, at least for the month of June, receipts had fallen off compared to the same period the previous year.

When the semiannual bill for the insurance on the inn arrived, she was concerned to learn that Dennis had increased the amount of the coverage, despite a staggering rise in the premium. She questioned her uncle about it, but his response was evasive.

53

"Don't you worry, Shannon," he said lightly. "That's *my* job."

"But Uncle Dennis"—she held up the statement from the insurance company—"how can the inn afford this?"

"The way building costs have skyrocketed, we can't afford not to increase the coverage," Dennis argued suavely. "Anyway, I think I've found a buyer for the inn and the parcel of land nearest the highway."

"A buyer?" she repeated numbly. "Who is it?"

"Deering Construction."

"Aren't they the ones who built that awful mobile-home park on the Hubbard farm?" Dennis nodded, and Shannon's voice rose with alarm as she recited details of that mismanaged project. "They took that lovely old place and created an eyesore! They stripped every single tree from the property, including those wonderful old maples, and they leveled it off, and filled in the pond—"

"They have no such intentions in this case," Dennis snapped.

Somewhat reassured, Shannon persisted, asking in a calmer tone, "Then what are their plans?"

Dennis swung angrily away from Shannon and walked to the windows behind his desk. In order to see out he had to open the blinds, and his hand was shaking so badly that he fumbled in his search for the cord before he finally found it.

The view from his office was not a very good one. All that he could see clearly was the utility area of the inn, but if he craned his neck, he could catch a glimpse of the tamarack-studded hillside where the chair lift began.

"If you honestly believe I'd allow Shagbark to be subdivided, under *any* circumstances," he said unevenly, "it shows how little you appreciate the seriousness with which I assumed responsibility for the management of all this." With one arm he made a proud, sweeping gesture that took in not only the MacLeod land but all the family heritage and the traditions of the inn.

Turning to glare at her, he exclaimed, "I resent your prying into matters that are still confidential! But I resent even more your insinuating that I'd permit the essential character of Shagbark to be destroyed! The least you can do is give me credit for wanting to justify my mother's confidence in me. Why, I'd cut off my right hand before I'd do anything to betray her trust!"

With relief Dennis noted that the guarded look had left Shannon's eyes and that they registered only sympathy for him. He released the cord and the blinds clattered down. Leaning forward and steadying himself with his hands outspread on the top of his desk, he spoke confidingly. "The Deerings plan to develop a country club. If they buy Shagbark, they'll remodel the main building and install a golf course and tennis courts, pro shops, a swimming pool."

The constraint between them had eased and, sighing, Dennis straightened until he stood erect. "So you see," he said softly, "it's all on the up-and-up and quite consistent with proper utilization of the acreage. There's nothing at all to worry about."

When Shannon silently left his office, Dennis smiled with satisfaction, for he knew that he'd successfully allayed his niece's fears.

Before the end of that summer Shannon had cause for bitter regret that she'd been swayed by Dennis's display of sentiment. If only she hadn't been so gullible, or if her uncle had been less persuasive, she might have pursued the question of the insurance. And if she'd done that, the disastrous events that had brought so much suffering to the Byrnes and the MacLeods might have been averted.

It was at a party in honor of Merry's nineteenth birthday that Shannon saw Adam again. She'd expected he would be Pamela's escort that evening, and she spent hours getting ready for the party. She'd gone through most of her wardrobe trying on one outfit after another, only to discard it in favor of yet another. In her agitated uncertainty she finally settled on a slinky black tube of a dress, but it took layers of foundation, blusher, eyeliner, several applications of mascara, and three shades of eye shadow before she felt she'd achieved the desired effect.

By the time she arrived at the Erskines' house, the party was in full swing. When she entered the living room, Merry was dancing with a lanky, bearded young man whose thinning hair, horn-rimmed glasses, and oddly serious smile gave him a bookish appearance. Shannon thought he looked like a youngish professor.

"I can't believe it's you, Shannon," Merry called over her partner's shoulder. "You look positively fabulous!"

Roger Warren was twenty-five and had never particularly noticed Shannon before, but that night he made a beeline to her side. He asked her to dance, and she considered this additional proof that she was capable of competing for Adam's attention on Pamela's ground.

The romance of the situation was minimal. Shannon didn't like Roger very much. He was almost too good-looking, and he was so polished and self-assured that she'd always thought he'd missed his calling by becoming an accountant. He reminded her of an advertisement for toothpaste or men's toiletries, and she suspected that, like an advertisement, he was mostly hype.

"I've been waiting for you to grow up, Shannon." Roger smiled meaningfully into her eyes. "I always knew you'd be a knockout." He had to repeat himself several times and finally shouted the compliment close to her ear in order to make himself heard above the din of the party, but Shannon believed his hackneyed line simply because she wanted to. She wanted so very much to think that it was true a man of Roger's age could see her as the woman she longed to be; the kind of woman she thought Adam wanted.

All the while she was dancing with Roger, she was scanning the room for Adam, and when Roger recognized that his audience wasn't properly appreciative, he was quick to cut his losses. He hurried Shannon to a corner of the living room where a bar and buffet had been set up, shoved a cup of punch into her hand, and went off in search of more cooperative game.

It was a warm evening, and with so many people jammed into the living room, the air was heavy with a mixture of smoke and perfumes and shaving lotions. The oppressive atmosphere made Shannon thirsty, and she quickly drank her punch. She was refilling her cup when Merry joined her.

"Have you seen LuAnne Follensbee?" Meredith's eyes sparkled with merriment. "It's only ten o'clock and she's already doing her striptease out on the patio."

"I haven't seen LuAnne," Shannon replied, "but I'd say that means your party is an unqualified success!"

"Yeah," Merry drawled as she surveyed the assortment of food on the buffet. "LuAnne doesn't usually get around to her repertoire of exotic numbers till midnight."

"I thought you didn't like LuAnne."

Merry nibbled on a cheese puff, selected a piece of

smoked salmon, and speared it with a toothpick before she answered. "To tell you the truth, I can't stand her."

"Then why did your parents invite her?"

"Because I added her name to the guest list. LuAnne makes me feel so superior," Merry unashamedly admitted. "Tonight she has some jock with her who claims he's on the track team at Purdue. Heck! To hear him tell it, he *is* the Purdue track team and LuAnne was bragging that he duck walks a mile every day. He's supposed to be a high-jump specialist, but if you ask me, he doesn't have enough sense to clear his throat."

Turning back to the table, Merry found a previously undiscovered plate of salmon. She pounced on it greedily.

"Who were you dancing with when I came in?" Shannon asked curiously. Whoever he was, Merry had certainly radiated contentment in his arms.

"That was Gil Rutherford. He's a friend of Adam's from Loyola."

Meredith was prone to going into great detail about the men she knew and, intrigued by her brevity, Shannon studied her friend with heightened interest.

It was apparent that in the past year Merry had taken her sister's advice and turned over a new leaf. The new Merry was svelte and impeccably groomed. Not a strand of her auburn hair was out of place, not a button was undone, and her lipstick toned beautifully with her dress. It was also apparent that Merry had no intention of elaborating on her description of Gil Rutherford, and in what she hoped was an offhand way Shannon asked, "Is Adam here tonight?"

Merry nodded and ate another piece of salmon. "The last I saw of him, he and Pamela were down in the rec room." She smiled the old Merry's wide, generous smile.

"Since she found out that Adam enjoys pocket billiards, my sister has become quite the pool shark."

Merry licked her fingers and dried them with a paper napkin. "Whew!" she exclaimed. "I'm a glutton for smoked salmon, but it's given me a terrible thirst."

Shannon poured out a cup of the fruit punch for Merry. "Have some of this," she suggested. "It's very refreshing."

For a moment Merry looked mystified, then she giggled and accepted the drink Shannon was offering her. "Great idea," she said. "How about you?"

Shannon fanned her flushed face with her hand. "I believe I will have another glass. Don't you think it's awfully warm in here?" She raised her cup and clinked it against Merry's before she drained it. "Mmmm," she enthused, "that's good! What's in it?"

"Oh, just cranberry juice and—er, things."

For some reason the vagueness of this response struck Shannon as being excruciatingly funny, and even when Merry excused herself she couldn't stop laughing. Merry said apologetically that she ought to speak to some of her other guests, but Gil Rutherford was dancing with Dixie Guthrie, and Shannon's impression was that Merry wanted to break up that twosome before it got any cozier. She decided that if she'd read her friend correctly, Merry was much more interested in Gil than she'd ever been in any of her other boyfriends.

She wondered uneasily if she was as transparent as her friend. Perhaps Merry had seen through her casual pose when she'd asked whether Adam was at the party, just as she'd seen through Merry's reticence on the subject of Gil Rutherford.

Aware for the first time of the beginnings of a headache, Shannon massaged her temple with perspiring fingers. Deciding that the faint, persistent throbbing had been brought on by the stifling heat in the living room, she threaded her way through the crowd toward the patio. A number of friends called to her and she returned their greetings, but she didn't stop to talk. Her smile felt as if it were glued on her face, and by the time she reached the patio her knees were so wobbly that she barely made it to a chair.

When Adam came upon her some time later, Shannon was still sitting in her unobtrusive spot behind a potted palm, inhaling deeply and trying to overcome a woozy, light-headed sensation.

Without preamble Adam asked, "Why are you hiding out here in the dark?"

"I'm not hiding," she demurred. "It's just that I'm not feeling very well."

The slurred complaint was followed by a hiccup, which prompted Adam to move a step nearer to her. His foot nudged her drink, and at the tinkling sound of the glass rolling across the concrete surface of the patio floor, he stopped in midstride. Following the sound, he recovered the cup, looked knowingly from it to Shannon, and inquired, "What have you been drinking?"

Shannon's lips moved to form an answer, but her tongue was thick and uncoordinated and it seemed to take forever before she managed to reply, "Only the fruit punch."

"*Only* the fruit punch!" Adam sounded amused now. "How much have you had?"

She held her head in her hands and tried very hard to remember. "I-I'm not sure. Two, maybe three, cups—"

"Or maybe four or five," he finished for her. "You little idiot! It's no wonder you lost track."

She made an effort to hold her head proudly erect and, failing miserably in the attempt, had to settle for asking in an aggrieved tone, "Are you implying that I'm drunk?"

"No, I'm not implying you're drunk," Adam countered in a mimicking singsong. "I'm saying it straight out. That punch is lethal. It's mostly vodka!"

He pulled her to her feet, and when she stumbled and fell against him, he slid an arm about her waist and propelled her away from the patio. She leaned on him, grateful for his support.

"Come on," he encouraged her gently when her legs threatened to give way beneath her. "Just a little farther now."

"Wh-where are you taking me?"

"I'm taking you home, Shannon."

Adam helped her into his car and fastened the seat belt around her. Her limbs were so rubbery and boneless, the upholstery of the bucket seat was so soft, Shannon thought she would sink right into it and keep on sinking until she disappeared. In her befuddled state it wasn't until they reached the billboard marking the turnoff to Eagles Nest that she realized they had passed Shagbark.

As if he'd read her mind, Adam stilled her protests before she could make them. "I don't think it would be a good idea to deliver you to your grandmother in your present condition. We'll get you sobered up first."

Leaving the drive, he pulled into a slot at the far corner of the parking lot; away from the other cars, away from the lights and pathways leading to the lobby. He eased Shannon out of the car and half carried, half walked her in the direction of one of the more secluded guest cottages.

In order to keep her from collapsing in a heap on the step, he had to use one hand to prop her against the wall while, with his other hand, he searched for his latchkey and unlocked the door. Throughout this procedure he was profanely condemning the maintenance staff because no one had gotten around to replacing the burned-out bulb in the carriage lamp on the porch.

At last the door was opened, and Adam released Shannon long enough to reach for the wall switch. Without him to hold her up her knees crumpled. She slid to the ground as limp as a rag doll, and this sent him into another stream of invective. His patience clearly at an end, he hefted her slight weight, slung her over his shoulder in a fireman's carry, and strode into the cottage, turning on lights as he went from entryway to living room to hallway.

The sudden rush of blood to her head roused Shannon enough that she squirmed about and tried to extricate herself from her ignominious position. Pummeling weakly at Adam's back with her fists, she cried, "Put me down," but her rebellion was ended by the openhanded swat Adam gave her bottom.

He'd purposely put more sound than fury into the slap, but it was accompanied by a muffled oath and the clipped order, "Keep still, damn it!"

From his tone Shannon knew he wouldn't hesitate over enforcing his command, and she obeyed it.

The combination of the sway of Adam's walk and the plaid design of the carpet swirling by was making her feel seasick, and she screwed her eyes tightly shut. Even when he set her on her feet again, she kept them closed, but she could tell by the chill smoothness of the tiled surface at her back that he'd carried her into the bathroom. It dawned on her that she was in the shower stall, and in the next instant Adam turned on the cold tap.

Her eyes opened wide with shock when the full force of

the water hit her. Choking and sputtering, she tried to escape the deluge.

"You're drowning me!" she gasped.

"That's not half of what you deserve." His hold on her was relentless.

"You're ruining my dress," she wailed.

Now that it was wet, the black satin of the garment clung even more revealingly to Shannon's curving figure, leaving little to the imagination, and his eyes roved ruthlessly over her tense young body.

"Nothing," he declared curtly, "could make that dress any worse than it is."

She drew in her breath to reply, but as soon as he saw she'd inhaled, Adam forced her head under the spray and held it there. When he allowed her to surface, her teeth were chattering and she was shivering, but she was also somewhat more alert. Her irritation over his criticism of her dress had been consumed by a larger anger, and it pleased her to see that, although he was standing outside of the stall, his sports jacket was being thoroughly drenched by the shower. She shook her hair out of her eyes to scowl at him.

"You look as if you can manage on your own now," Adam observed. "I'll leave a robe for you on the hook by the door."

The stall door clicked shut, and he left her alone, returning in a few seconds with the promised robe.

"As long as you're in there," he called briskly, "do us both a favor and wash your face."

Shannon's face was scrubbed and shiny when she emerged from the bathroom, and she was sober enough to be fully conscious that she was in Adam's private apartment. She was also sober enough to be embarrassed as she walked across the living room toward him. She was swamped by the voluminous folds of his white terry cloth robe, and she felt as fragile as an eggshell. Aware of Adam watching her, she cautiously placed one small, bare foot in front of the other in order to keep from staggering. When she reached the sofa, she perched on the very edge of it and wished she could vanish. She wished the ground would simply open up and swallow her.

Removing a high-heeled sandal from the pocket of the sweat shirt he'd changed into, Adam dropped it in her lap. "I could only find one of your shoes," he said.

"I think I lost the other one on the way to the car," she confessed. Her face was hot with color, and she couldn't bring herself to meet his eyes. She couldn't bear it if he was laughing at her.

"Coffee?" he laconically inquired.

She heard the suppressed amusement in his voice and took the steaming mug he held out for her without replying. She wrapped her icy fingers around it and was comforted by its warmth.

Adam poured some coffee for himself before he sat at the opposite end of the couch. Shannon risked a glance at him and, since he was watching her, he caught her in the act.

"Well," he toasted, smiling, "here's to crime."

Her eyes shied away from him, and she drank her coffee. For a time neither of them spoke.

As he refilled her cup Adam remarked softly, "You look much nicer without all that makeup."

More disconcerted than ever by this faint praise, Shannon retreated to the security of cool formality and restricted her reply to a polite, "Thank you."

"I wonder why the young are always so all-fired anxious to grow up," he mused.

"You're not exactly Methuselah," she retorted stiffly.

"No," he conceded. "And you're not exactly a child, but I've decided you need someone to take you in hand before you find yourself in a situation you can't handle."

She buried her face in the cloud of vapor rising from her cup and didn't respond.

"Furthermore," he drawled, "I've decided it should be me."

Shannon turned her startled face toward Adam, smiling elatedly when she saw that he was serious.

"Don't let it go to your head," he teased. "It's only because I think you'd be too much for most men to manage."

Without realizing she'd changed position, she found herself sliding along the couch to be closer to him. He stopped her before she could touch him, however, holding her at arm's length with his hands hard on her shoulders.

"Not so fast, Shannon," he commanded. Although his grip on her was punishing, his eyes lingered on the soft enticement of her lips before they smiled into hers. "I told you once before that you're an apt pupil, and this is your chance to prove it. Lesson number one is that men prefer to do the chasing."

She felt honor bound to dispute this statement, but she'd barely opened her mouth when the dark flash of Adam's eyes silenced her.

"I'm aware that according to feminist rhetoric it's bad form to make such distinctions between the sexes." He shrugged carelessly. "Maybe they're right. Maybe it's atavistic to believe that men have been the hunters for too long to get their kicks out of being the quarry. But if that belief makes me a throwback to the cave, so be it!"

In a small voice Shannon explained, "I only wanted to kiss you."

"I want the same thing," Adam grudgingly admitted. "And that's the problem. At this moment I want to kiss you *too* much. Under the circumstances it could be hazardous.

"For me or for you?"

"For both of us."

He let go of her arms and his hand moved caressingly over her throat to her chin, tilting her face so that the light fell on it. Smiling reminiscently, he recalled that when he'd seen her at the party, in her clingy black dress with her face so theatrically made up, she'd reminded him of a little girl playing dress-up. Without the cosmetics her skin was as flawless and fine-grained as an apple blossom, and so translucent that he could see the warm fluctuation of color in her cheeks. Because her complexion was so smooth and unlined, she looked younger but, at the same time, was more womanly.

He traced the tender curve of her mouth with the ball of his thumb, and when he felt her tremble under his touch, his smile faded and he pulled his hands away from her. Jamming his fists into his pants pockets, he got to his feet to put a safer distance between them.

"Lesson number two," he said firmly, "is that if we're going to see one another, I'll set the pace. And *I* say we take it slow and easy; one step at a time."

CHAPTER FIVE

That night was the real beginning for them. Seven years later, viewing it with the clarity of hindsight while the nippy September dark stole into the gazebo, Shannon likened the rest of that summer to a roller-coaster ride.

For her, being with Adam had been like a climb toward some unseen, as yet unknown, pinnacle. The ascent itself was fraught with excitement. Lured on by the delights that might be waiting for her when she finally reached the summit, she'd lived on her nerves, seething at a fever pitch of expectancy. But when she'd arrived at the peak, the heady thrill of triumph was all too brief. Balanced on the knife-edged intensity of her emotions, she'd been unable to maintain her poise, and when it was too late to turn back, she'd discovered that all that lay ahead was a wild, downhill ride that had ended in harsh reality. She'd been swept along by circumstances that were beyond her control, and she was helpless to stop the fearful plunge.

In retrospect it was difficult to understand how she could have been so blind. Whenever they chanced to meet, Edwin Byrne had been unfailingly polite, but Shannon sensed he disapproved of Adam's spending so much time with her. Her uncle, on the other hand, was violently opposed to Adam. As the summer wore on and each business day brought its quota of dunning letters from the inn's creditors, Dennis came to look upon her as the enemy. Eventually even her grandmother had joined the opposition and tried to discourage her from seeing Adam.

At the time, though, she'd been so beguiled by Adam, so caught up in the joy of being in love with him, that she'd ignored the danger signs.

They'd spent most of their free time together. They took the Eagles Nest houseboat out on the river. They swam and fished. They bicycled and played tennis. They went to parties and ballgames, to barbecues, and to the itinerant carnivals that visited Galena. They went to square dances at the Palace Ballroom and watched every Bogart film on the late show on television.

Adam showed her an album of his photographs and tried taking some pictures of her, but he gave it up after he'd developed the first roll of film. When she asked him why he was dissatisfied with her as a model, he said bluntly, "You're too big a ham." At her insistence he finally let her look at the prints, and when she saw how revealing they were, she decided it was just as well Adam had decided not to take any more. In each of the pictures she was laughing, radiant with happiness and obviously in love.

Throughout that summer they talked a lot and laughed a lot, and if there was anything to mar Shannon's happiness, it was her disappointment that Adam was so undemonstrative. But if he rarely kissed her, he teased her affectionately, more often than not about her habit of going barefoot and her tendency to forget where she'd left her shoes.

"You lose shoes the way some women lose earrings," he said. "I can't figure out why it's always just *one* of them."

And sometimes he flattered her, in a bantering, back-handed kind of way.

"Did you know, Shannon," he informed her one humid evening when she'd worn her hair up, "that in the Orient the nape of a woman's neck is considered a highly erotic part of her anatomy."

Shannon's heart skipped a beat and she held her breath, paralyzed with anticipation, while Adam leaned so close that his breath fanned her skin. He ran his forefinger lightly along the side of her neck to the spot where her jawline joined her ear and she shivered with pleasure at his touch.

"And if it's a long neck," he went on huskily, "then it's especially arousing."

"Oh, God," Shannon prayed silently, fervently, "please don't let him stop."

But Adam straightened and his hand fell away from her. "I just thought you should know," he finished affably. "If you ever decide you want to be a sex symbol, you can move to Japan and become an overnight sensation."

Another time, when they were lazing in the sun on the poolside deck at Eagles Nest, Adam complimented her on her legs.

"Small girls tend to have short, stumpy little legs," he said thoughtfully. "But yours are long and gorgeous."

Shannon was lying on her back, and she raised one leg until her toes pointed toward the sky. Wriggling her toes, she moved her head this way and that, studying her leg critically from different angles. By now she knew Adam well enough that she didn't take his accolade too seriously, and she replied modestly, "They're legs like any others. They're a matched set and they're certainly long enough for me. They reach all the way from my hips to my ankles."

"But such hips! And what ankles!" Adam, too, was studying her leg. "And your thigh is a thing of beauty. It's so round and firm, so golden brown and delectable."

Shannon giggled at this extravagance and exclaimed, "You make me sound like Chicken-in-a-Basket!"

"Ah, yes, my little chickadee!" Adam persisted, straight-faced. "I could compose a lyric to your legs. I could write a melody to your mouth, a sonnet to your skin—"

"I much prefer *your* legs," Shannon interjected. "They're so muscular and strong, so knobby-kneed and handsomely hairy." She was holding her sides with laughter as she ventured, "I could write a haiku to your hair—"

Rolling lithely to his feet, Adam picked her up and carried her, kicking and squealing but still laughing, to the side of the pool, where he held her out over the water.

"No, Adam, don't!" she shrieked when his arms dipped, threatening to drop her.

"Knobby-kneed, am I?" he growled. His eyes shone wickedly. Her efforts to hang onto him were futile, and he tossed her into the water, diving in after her when she surfaced. For the rest of that hot Sunday afternoon they swam and ducked each other and frolicked in the pool, as carefree as children.

Their relationship continued in this platonic, lighthearted way through the first week of July. Shannon was hopelessly in love with Adam, and she was happier than she'd ever been. At the same time, she was greedy for more. Adam had more zest, more passion, for living than anyone she'd ever known, yet he never channeled any of his sexual passion in her direction. She yearned for greater intima-

70

cies and was more than a little frightened by her yearnings. She wanted his treatment of her to change, yet she wanted to maintain the status quo. But most of all she was puzzled by Adam's restraint. She began to worry that he regarded her as a younger sister, or as a friend, or that he didn't really care for her at all.

If Merry hadn't been so involved with Gil Rutherford, Shannon might have asked her advice. Until that summer Merry and she had always shared their secrets. But Merry had changed, and she had too. They were no longer confidantes.

With each day that passed, Shannon's frustration grew —until one night in the middle of July when Adam's good-night kiss blended into another, and another, and still another, and all at once they were sprawled on the front porch swing with the demanding hardness of his body moving urgently, as if he were trying to immerse himself in her softness, and kissing was not enough to satisfy either of them. Both of them were trembling when Adam's lips trailed hotly from Shannon's mouth to the delicate hollows at the base of her throat.

"I agree with the Japanese," he muttered hoarsely. "Your long beautiful neck is unbearably sexy."

He undid the top buttons of her blouse and impatiently pushed the collar aside so that his mouth could explore more intimately across the arc of her collarbone and down to the soft swell of her breasts. He lingered at the shadowy valley between them, inhaling her fragrance, wanting to see and touch and know more of her—wanting all of her.

Finally, tensing with self-denial, Adam raised his head, rolled off of her and onto his side, keeping her folded close in his arms.

"Congratulations," he said thickly, rubbing his cheek

71

against hers. "You've successfully completed lessons three and four."

"Do I get good marks?" she whispered.

Adam laughed shakily. "The highest for three. For four, only so-so. But it's not entirely your fault."

Shannon tilted her head back to look dazedly up at his face. "I don't understand."

"I neglected to tell you that at that level, a bit more student participation is customary."

"In that case," she murmured seductively, "maybe my teacher will let me take a make-up exam."

She heard the sharp intake of his breath as he fought for control, and then, as if the provocation were too great to withstand, he groaned, "I think that just might be arranged."

When Adam kissed her this time, hungrily parting her lips and ravishing her mouth, Shannon gladly let her instincts show her a more expressive means of demonstrating her love for him. Luxuriating in the silken warmth of his hair-roughened skin, relishing the supple flexing of muscles in his shoulders, her eager fingers searched and discovered, touched and caressed, until they reached for his belt buckle and Adam stopped her, locking her so tightly in his arms that she could scarcely breathe.

"I love you, Adam," she cried, and immediately felt his withdrawal.

Sighing deeply, Adam moved away from her and began buttoning his shirt. His hands were unsteady, but his expression was so remote that she felt chilled by it.

"I-I suppose I shouldn't have said that," Shannon stammered.

"No, you shouldn't," Adam agreed flatly, "but then, we've both done things tonight that we shouldn't have."

* * *

After that night one dreary day followed another without Adam calling Shannon or stopping at Shagbark to see her. A week had gone by before she chanced to meet Merry in town and learned that he was going out with Pamela again.

"A friend of Adam's is a partner in some new disco near Dubuque. Adam took Pamela to the opening on Saturday," Merry divulged. "Then last night they went on the dinner cruise on one of the riverboats."

Although Shannon had tried to accustom herself to the idea that Adam was seeing someone else, she found she was totally unprepared to hear about it. Blinking rapidly to hold back tears, she pressed her lips together to keep from crying out, but it was impossible to conceal her sudden pallor.

"I'm sorry, Shannon," Merry sympathized. "I guess you must go for Adam in a big way."

For an instant, Shannon considered dissembling, but she didn't.

"I'm in love with him," she confided. Oddly enough, it was a relief to have made this admission.

"And Adam?" Merry asked softly. "How does he feel about you?"

Shannon's uncertainty was reflected in the clouded violet of her eyes. "For a while I thought he was attracted to me, but now I'm not sure."

"Doesn't it strike you that the heavy-handed way he broke off with you is out of character for Adam?" Merry's expression was thoughtful. "He must like you, otherwise he'd never have tolerated your company for six weeks. So why didn't he let you down gently? Why did he start up

73

again with the one woman he can be *sure* you'd find out about?"

"I wish I knew, Merry," Shannon replied brokenly.

"Maybe he cares for you too much," Merry surmised. "It's possible that Adam doesn't want to become seriously involved with anyone. He and Gil have been friends since they were in prep school, but Gil told me he *still* doesn't know Adam very well. He says Adam's always been a loner."

Shannon nodded. Adam was a terribly private person. For six weeks she'd seen him almost daily, they'd spent a great deal of time together, yet with the exception of superficial details she knew almost nothing of a personal nature about him.

She knew he liked to travel to out-of-the-way places—the more remote the better. She knew he took his coffee black, his steak rare, and that he rarely ate desserts. She knew that he enjoyed *Doonesbury,* Dickens, and Twain; that he preferred Bach and the Beatles to Tchaikovsky or Wagner; that in addition to Bogart he admired the contributions to film-making of Stanley Kubrick and Alfred Hitchcock. She knew that Adam's energy was boundless, so much so that he became restless and grouchy if he had to remain inactive for any length of time—unless he happened to be fishing. Then he was content to sit motionless for hours on end.

One early morning when they were fishing, she'd asked him about his medallion. It was an ankh on a heavy silver chain, and he wore it always.

"I've had it since I was a kid," he replied shortly.

"But isn't that kind of cross symbolic of something?" she inquired.

"It's supposed to represent life—both this life and the eternal life to come."

"Is that what it means to you?"

"No," he said, frowning repressively at her. "To me it represents freedom—particularly freedom from being cross-examined by little girls who are too curious for their own good!"

Shannon hadn't questioned Adam any further about the ankh. His frown and his clipped response had prevented that. But they hadn't stopped her from fearing what the medallion symbolized to him.

When she said good-bye to Shannon, Meredith was feeling suspiciously sentimental. She and Gil were in love, and she wanted the whole world to bask in the glow of their happiness. As she walked the few blocks to her home she told herself that Adam Byrne was the worst kind of fool if he didn't reciprocate Shannon's love for him. And for two cents she'd be more than willing to tell him so.

The chance to keep this resolution came sooner than Merry could have foreseen. Less than a week later she and Gil arranged to attend a Renaissance Fair in Freeport with Adam and Pamela. As usual Pamela kept the rest of them waiting while she finished getting dressed. Merry and Gil were working a crossword puzzle while they waited, but Adam was on edge. He kibitzed for a bit, and when he became bored with that, he prowled about the room until Gil's concentration was disrupted.

"What's wrong with you lately, Adam?" he asked.

"Nothing," Adam growled.

"Well, something's bugging you," Gil insisted. "You haven't been yourself all week. I know you're not the most patient of men, but I've never seen you so restless and irritable."

"At the moment the only thing bugging me is *you,* buddy-boy."

The two men scowled at one another, and Merry gathered her courage and piped up, "Don't worry, Gil, no one ever died of what's ailing Adam."

Adam's frown deepened as he turned on Merry. "Just what is that supposed to mean?"

"You're a big boy now," Merry coolly retorted. "Surely you can figure it out for yourself. Or do you want me to draw you a diagram?"

"Skip the sarcasm, Merry," Adam drawled, "and stop trying to be mysterious. I never was any good at puzzles."

"Then I'll give you a clue you can't go wrong with. Your ailment is a four-letter word—"

"Shame on you, Merry," Gil scolded her mockingly. "You know your mother won't allow you to use four-letter words."

Raising her voice to drown out Gil's teasing, Merry continued mutinously, "Beginning with *L* and defined as 'a deep, tender devotion or attachment.' It's often associated with desire and passion."

Adam was obviously stunned by Merry's assertion, and Gil spoke up. "So you think it's *love* that's bothering him." He smiled benignly at Adam. "Maybe you're right at that. He's lost his patience, he's lost his appetite, he's lost his temper, he's even lost his sense of humor! But don't leave me in suspense any longer. Aren't you going to tell me who the object of his desire and passion is?"

"By all means, Merry, let's not leave anyone in suspense," Adam grimly enjoined. "Tell us the end of this fairy tale."

76

"Very well," she agreed pertly. "Since you insist, I'll give you another clue. The first name begins with an *S.* For the scholars among us, in the ancient Celtic this name was applied to 'still waters.' "

"As in 'run deep'?" Gil looked perturbed. "This is a tough one," he complained. "Do I get a gold star if I get it right?"

"Do you want another clue?" asked Merry.

Livid with anger, Adam shouted, "No!"

"Well, you're going to get one anyway," she declared. "The first initial and surname are an anagram for *Damocles,* which seems to be the way you'd define love, Adam. You seem to think love puts a person in imminent danger, like the sword of the same name."

Gil dashed to the writing desk and scribbled "Damocles" on a notepad. "What the hell is an anagram?" he asked. "Isn't that where you make up a new word from the letters of another one?"

"That's right, Gil," Merry praised sweetly. "You're a constant source of amazement to me."

"Hey, I've got it!" Gil exclaimed. "S. MacLeod," he chortled. "It's your little friend Shannon!"

Too furious to reply, Adam turned on his heel, stalked out of the living room, and slammed out of the house. But by the following night he had resumed seeing Shannon.

It was several weeks before Adam told Shannon about his and Merry's Donnybrook. By then he was able to see the humor in the audacious way Merry had championed Shannon's cause. They even laughed about it.

When Mr. and Mrs. Erskine made the formal announcement of their daughter's engagement to Gil Rutherford, Adam remarked dryly, "With a wife like Merry, Gil's going to have his hands full. After seeing her in action, he probably decided he'd better keep her in his corner, no matter what the cost!"

On the morning after Merry and Gil's engagement party, Adam took Shannon out in the houseboat. They drifted lazily downstream, and Adam fished while she lay in the sun on the cabin roof, watching him and wishing she could suspend time, or at least slow its passage.

It was the second week of September, and it seemed that one day summer had been in full, glorious bloom, then, overnight, there was a hint of autumn in the air. In only ten days she would be leaving for Minneapolis while Adam returned to Chicago for his second year of law school, and she felt a heavy sadness. It was as if she'd had some premonition that whatever affection Adam felt for her would fade with the season.

On that Sunday, however, summer had summoned all of its strength for one dying effort, and the day was fiercely hot. At noon they anchored in a quiet backwater where a sultry heat-haze shimmered above the torpid surface of the water. A sluggish little breeze rustled through the trees that lined the shore and then was still, and the incessant hum of the cricket-song seemed deafening.

As the sun had climbed higher in the sky Adam had stripped until he wore only cutoff jeans that rode low on his narrow hips and a battered baseball cap that shaded his eyes. When the anchor was set, he dove into the water and swam around the boat for a few minutes to cool off.

Try as she might, Shannon could not prevent herself from watching Adam. The sight of him knifing through the water and emerging from the river onto the boat deck with water running in rivulets down his flat belly, with his hair gleaming sable dark, his skin bronzed by the sun and burnished by the droplets of water that remained from his swim, was too commanding to ignore.

When he bent over the portable icebox to find a cold drink, she continued to stare at him, relishing the lithe angularity of his hard brown torso and long powerful legs.

Waving the can of beer he'd chosen, Adam called, "Do you want one of these?"

Shannon shook her head. Her throat felt so tight she doubted she could swallow.

He shrugged negligently, popped the can open, and drank deeply before he climbed the ladder to the roof where she was sunbathing. Holding the frost-beaded can against his forehead, he dropped down beside her.

His skin was damp and sleek as satin, and she wanted to run her hand over the muscular symmetry of his back and along the lean, ridged surface of his rib cage. The longing to touch him was so overwhelming that it required a conscious exercise of will not to do so. Her hand had actually moved toward him involuntarily when he shifted position to finish his beer, and the ankh swung loose for a moment before it was partially hidden by the dark mat of hair on his chest.

In contrast with the warm copper-gold of his skin, the medallion's silvered luster was cold, and Shannon was reminded that it signified Adam's determination to remain a free spirit. She realized how much she disliked the ankh, and she was afraid that Adam would read her aversion to it in her eyes. She turned over so that she lay prone, with her face away from him, clenching her teeth and curling her fingers into her palms.

"You're getting sunburned," Adam commented idly. "Give me your sunscreen and I'll put some on your back for you."

"No," she answered tightly. If he were to touch her just now, she knew she'd make a complete fool of herself.

His hand curved about her shoulder, and he felt her tense with resistance to his gesture of concern.

"What's eating you today?" he asked. His voice was gentle, as was his touch. "You've hardly said two words all morning."

"The summer's almost over, and I can't bear it," she burst out shakily. "After we go back to school, I won't see you again."

"Of course you will," he said evenly. "We'll both be home over Christmas."

"It won't be the same," she cried.

"Probably not," Adam agreed lightly. "Nothing ever is." For a few seconds he was silent, and she sensed that he was watching her. At last he said softly, "I'm flattered you want things to go on between us, Shannon, and I'll miss you, but we haven't any choice." He sighed. "What would you like us to do?"

"I don't know," she lied. She wanted to be with Adam. She wanted him to kiss her. She wanted him to make love to her. She was achingly aware of his body so close to hers and, with every fiber of her being, she simply wanted him—in any way, in *every* way that he would permit.

The small space that separated them was suddenly charged with reciprocal awareness, and Adam's grip on her shoulder tightened convulsively. Recognizing her need, he pulled her over so that she lay on her side facing him, and his eyes sought the smoky turbulence of hers.

"Do you think I don't want you too?" he demanded. His voice was vibrant with suppressed desire. "Have you any idea how hard it's been to see you every day and *not* seduce you?"

Her body yearned for his, and she moved until the length of his thighs was so close to her own that she was able to feel how tautly controlled he was.

"How can it be seduction when I want you so much?" she whispered.

"You're too young to know what you want," he countered dismissively.

"I'm not!" she protested. "All I want is to be with you."

"With both of us still in school? Be practical, honey!" he exclaimed derisively. "You know I'd refuse to ask my father for financial help, even if he wasn't having such a rough go of it with Eagles Nest just now."

"I am being practical," she brazenly insisted. "I could get a job. I could even work part time and transfer my credits so that I could go back to college in the spring."

She saw the conflicting emotions in his expression as desire battled with reason, as need warred with caution, and when she pressed her cheek to his chest, she heard the wild thudding of his heart. She moved even closer to him, and this time she felt the impassioned surge of his body against hers.

Shamelessly she pleaded, "I don't require much space, and I wouldn't eat very much. It wouldn't cost you anything at all to keep me."

"Only my sanity," Adam muttered hoarsely.

In the next instant his arms crushed her to him, and his mouth was hard and demanding as it claimed the yielding softness of hers. His hands were hot and impatient as they moved over her back, following the fragile slope of her shoulder blades to find the fastening of the halter top of her bathing suit, releasing the knot and peeling the halter and the briefs roughly away from her, baring her body for his fevered caresses.

Her own mouth was as demanding as his. It opened enticingly, inviting the sweet penetration of his tongue, and her hands were equally impatient as they gripped his shoulders and explored the rugged planes and angles of his body. She hugged him to her so tightly that the rough weave of his cutoffs grazed her skin, but when she felt the medallion scrape painfully across her breast, she loosened her hold on him and tried to work the chain over his head.

His awareness of Shannon's discomfort enabled Adam to make one final, desperate bid for control. He pushed her away and started to get to his feet, but he couldn't stop himself from looking at her. In a single glance he saw that her body was like a cameo—all soft amber and ivory, all warm coral and wild honey. He was arrested by her sun-washed loveliness, and his eyes were dark and fathomless as they strayed over her, but she made no attempt to cover herself.

He knelt beside her and his hand moved toward her. His touch was featherlight as he traced the line of demarcation between her sunkissed parts and the secret, paler places her bathing suit had concealed. His hand charted the graceful curve from her hip to her waist, and he marveled at how delicately she was fashioned, marveled at the contrast between the milky fairness of her skin and the swarthiness of his. Entranced by the velvety-softness of her skin, his hand moved to cup her breast, and the last frail vestige of his control snapped.

"Forgive me," he said, and his voice rang with rueful acceptance. When Shannon thought about it later, it seemed to her that he'd been asking her pardon because it was beyond him to resist the temptation to take what she was offering him, but in that moment she was incapable of thought, for in a dazzling motion that made her senses reel, Adam removed the medallion, tossed it aside, and lowered his head to kiss the small abrasion the ankh had made.

Utterly abandoned now, Shannon exulted in the slow fire of his lips moving over the creamy rise of her breast. He paused to test the ripeness of the nipple and found it was already sweetly engorged and pushing upward to meet the erotic sorcery of his mouth.

Once again his hands trailed over her, stopping to verify her excitement in the pulses that raced in her throat before they swept boldly to her thighs. His fingers skillfully tantalized her, probing for and finding the fires of her passion, stroking her moist, tender flesh until her whole body seemed to vibrate and she arched deliriously into the intimacy of his touch.

Wave after wave of pleasure washed over her, each one more delicious than the one before, until she felt she would die from the sheer ecstasy of it.

Then, unexpectedly, the stillness of the air was shattered by the roar of an approaching motor. They had sufficient warning to break apart before a speedboat towing a water skier rounded a point of land to enter the inlet where they were anchored. By the time the intruders were near enough to see them clearly, Adam had stationed himself by the railing to cut off their view of Shannon, and she had managed to pull on her beach coat.

The speedboat made a wide circuit of the inlet and, with a cacophony of apologies and ribald quips from its occupants, was gone as quickly as it had appeared.

Without speaking to her, without so much as glancing in her direction, Adam bounded down the ladder to weigh anchor and start the motor. His face was shuttered and detached as he worked, and although he maintained his moody silence after they had tied up at the Eagles Nest dock, Shannon was rejoicing, for he'd forgotten to retrieve his medallion.

She knew she should have returned the ankh to him, but she didn't. She picked it up and covertly tucked it into her beach bag, beneath her towel and sunglasses and tanning cream. She carried it back to Shagbark with her, and even when Adam looked at her curiously, wondering at her composure, she never mentioned it to him.

And this unthinking act of dishonesty proved to be her downfall.

CHAPTER SIX

Shannon had never been able to bring any order to her recollections about the night of the fire. It had been at least five years since she'd actively thought about it, but her memories still lacked any real coherence. The enormity of the events of that night was too great. Too much had happened too fast, and she had come away from it wounded, with only a confused jumble of impressions.

The most vivid images were of Adam. His face reflecting the warm glow of the flames dancing in the hearth. His austere features sharpened and suffused with passion while he'd made love to her with a hunger so vast she'd thought it would never be filled. The chiaroscuro effect of firelight leaping over his body, gilding his skin ruddy-gold. Her hands touching him, loving him, eager to please him. His hands on her, and—oh, God!—his lips.

For years she'd been haunted by recurring dreams in which Adam was holding her, kissing her, loving her. She'd awakened from them crying at her deprivation.

Now she remembered that his arms had been strong and sure about her and his touch warm and sensuous. He'd tenderly unlocked the mysteries of her body, skillfully arousing her mindless response. She remembered the delicious weight of him and the silky glide of his body, moving slowly at first, then faster, and finally with primitive urgency. She remembered the sound of his voice whispering endearments and urging her onward to new, unexplored heights. And, at the moment of release, the deep-throated growl of triumph that seemed to come from the very center of his being.

Afterward he'd held her and touched her possessively and said, "You're not a child any longer, Shannon. You're a woman—*my* woman!"

It wasn't until later that she'd realized he'd never said he loved her.

She had. "I love you, Adam," she'd cried. "I love you, love you, love you." Over and over again she'd repeated it. Like a litany.

She remembered that the rumble of thunder had startled her out of a deep sleep in the predawn hours of the morning. When she discovered that Adam's side of the bed was empty, she called for him and searched the cottage. The stab of alarm she had felt when she found that he was gone was mild compared to the shock of the ugly surprises that were in store for her.

She pulled on the first garment that came to hand—Adam's terry cloth robe—and hurried outside. That was when she noticed the broad, bloodred streak that illuminated the darkness of the northern horizon. Still somewhat disoriented because she'd awakened in a strange place, she'd stared dumbly at the sky for some time before she recognized that the eerie phenomenon was caused by a fire and, from the dimensions of the blaze of color, a huge one. She knew the area with the familiarity of a lifetime, and she knew that the only building in the vicinity of the fire that was large enough to burn so brightly was Shagbark.

She'd never understood why she'd reacted so irrationally to that knowledge. There were people and cars and telephones at the lodge at Eagles Nest, but it hadn't occurred to her to ask anyone for help. Instead she set off on foot. By following the route of the highway, it was four miles to the inn, but she hadn't followed the highway. She'd gone cross-country.

Perhaps it was panic that drove her, or a homing instinct. Or perhaps, subconsciously, she had already summed up the danger signals that she had ignored until that night.

While the storm raged about her, she scrambled uphill and down. She waded swampy gullies and jogged across grassy fields. Through woods and brush she ran and walked and ran again.

The robe was far too long for her, and when the hem became damp it dragged heavily at her legs, tripping her. All she had to light her way were intermittent flashes of lightning, and she often stumbled over stones and exposed roots and other unseen obstacles. At times the thunder was so close that it seemed simultaneous with the lightning; so close that it seemed to shake the very ground. But there was only a spattering of rain.

The wind whipped around her so strongly that she had to lean into it in order to make any headway. It blinded her and whistled past her ears until they ached. It tore at the robe and tossed her hair into a wild tangle of witchlocks.

Long before she reached the inn her feet were scratched and bruised, so that she was limping in her thin-soled slippers, and her bewilderment was compounded by a bone-deep weariness.

The wind died down, leaving the moisture-laden air

stagnant and heavy, but the rain did not begin in earnest until she arrived at the inn. From her vantage point at the top of the ski run, what remained of Shagbark was like a stage set from Dante's *Inferno*. The gutted ruins of the inn still smoldered, and occasionally flames erupted from the bowels of the rubble, sending showers of sparks skyward. A pall of smoke blanketed the scene, and the rain only emphasized the acrid stink of destruction.

The fire department was beginning mopping-up operations, but emergency vehicles of every description clogged the parking area, red lights turning and winking. Fire and police personnel rushed about, their progress unimpeded by clusters of onlookers who were contained behind the police barricade.

Shannon recalled wandering through the crowd and hearing speculative snatches of conversation.

"With the power failure, they couldn't use the water supply. They had to wait for the pumper truck."

"I heard it was the wiring."

". . . something in the kitchen."

"Naw! It was lightning that started it."

". . . burn, baby, burn!"

"What are you, anyway? Some kind of ghoul? It's a lucky thing no one was inside—"

"Yep! It was set, sure as shootin'!"

"Chief Larkin thinks it was arson, but thinking and proving are two different things."

After she heard that, with each step she took, some incriminating piece of the jigsaw puzzle clicked into place. If the fire had been started deliberately, the case against her uncle was a strong one. There were his gambling debts, the dunning letters, and the weak financial position of the inn. There was Dennis's obsession that the Byrnes must

88

never acquire Shagbark. There was his despondency when Deering Construction had reneged on their offer to purchase.

And the most damning evidence of all was the fact that the premium on the fire insurance was past due. The grace period would expire in mid-September and, to the best of her knowledge, short of a miracle, there was no way that Dennis could hope to raise enough cash to pay it.

Shannon's suspicions about her uncle shocked her out of her daze, but she was still wandering aimlessly about when Dennis appeared from out of the crowd to seize her arm roughly and drag her to a quieter spot.

"Where the hell have you been?" he asked irately. "Your grandmother has been worried sick about you."

Ignoring his question, Shannon confronted him with the rumors she'd heard.

Dennis nodded, corroborating the gossip. "It's true that Chief Larkin is investigating the possibility of arson, and in my opinion the most likely suspect is Adam Byrne."

"No," Shannon countered heatedly. "Adam would never do such a thing."

"How can you be so sure of that?" Dennis asked sharply.

"I just am. Adam's not the kind of man who'd ever resort to anything underhanded—"

"Suppose you let an expert tell you what kind of man Adam Byrne is," Dennis angrily interrupted. "He's no better than the rest of his clan. He resents the fact that Shagbark is MacLeod land, and he'll stop at nothing—up to and including arson—to run us off! Surely you don't believe that you're the reason he's been nosing around here all summer?"

"Yes, Uncle Dennis," Shannon quietly replied. "That's exactly what I believe."

"Then you're a bigger fool than I thought!" her uncle exclaimed caustically. "I'm convinced Adam started the fire, and what's more, I intend to inform Chief Larkin."

"That's impossible," Shannon stated emphatically. "Adam was with me tonight, almost *all* night."

Outraged by his niece's admission, Dennis's breath hissed between his teeth and he struck Shannon. He hit her so forcefully that she staggered away from him and almost fell, and when she regained her balance, his face was contorted to a mask of hatred.

"You little tramp!" His voice was menacing, and when he took a step toward her his expression was so belligerent that she cautiously retreated. "Think what it will do to your grandmother if she finds out—"

"Please, Uncle Dennis, it isn't like that," she hastily corrected him. "Adam and I were married yesterday afternoon."

"Married!" he echoed incredulously. "Of all the dimwitted—Both of you still have years of school ahead of you."

"Lots of married couples attend college, and they manage very well."

"More of them don't!"

"Well, *we* will," Shannon said determinedly.

Dennis regarded her narrowly. "This is awfully sudden, isn't it? And just to go off and get married without telling anyone—it's so hole-and-corner." He scrutinized her more closely. "Shannon," he inquired nastily, "are you pregnant?"

"No," she replied steadily, "but if I were, I'd be proud that I was having Adam's child. The only reason we got married as we did is because of the bad feeling between our families. We thought it would cause less friction if we presented all of you with an accomplished fact. I would have liked a traditional wedding, but the ceremony isn't important. All that matters is that I love Adam and he loves me."

"I think not," Dennis smugly retorted. "Not any longer." He smiled slyly. "I saw Adam less than half an hour ago, and when I finished with him he seemed to have the idea that your only reason for spending so much time with him this summer was to help me set him up. And now I see why he was so easy to con. After all, not only are you his alibi for tonight, he thinks you gave me his calling card."

Dennis patted his jacket pockets, removed the ankh from one, and held it out for her inspection.

"I can see you recognize it," he said, "and so will Chief Larkin when I tell him I found it near the inn just after the fire broke out." He laughed maliciously. "It's rather an inspired story, if I do say so myself."

The sight of the medallion electrified Shannon. Without taking her eyes off it, she demanded, "Where did you get that?"

"Why, from the drawer in your desk where you left it." Dennis shrugged complacently. "Having gone this far, I may as well admit that I told Adam you've been my accomplice in framing him for arson, so you can understand why he now considers you a cross between Mata Hari and Delilah."

"He believed you?"

"My dear child, after the way his mother treated his father and him, naturally he believed me!"

Drawing herself up to her full height, Shannon declared, "It won't work, Uncle Dennis. If you dare to accuse Adam publicly, I'll tell the authorities everything I know about the inn's financial problems. Don't forget, I know how near you are to bankruptcy, and about your gambling. I know about the insurance, and I know how desperate you've been to salvage something from the business."

Dennis's self-satisfied smirk faded. "You're so besotted with Adam Byrne, no one would take your word."

"They wouldn't have to. You aren't the only one who has hard evidence."

"You're bluffing." Dennis's voice was firm, but his hands were unsteady. "You have no proof."

"Haven't I?" Now it was Shannon who smiled. "The only way you'll find out is by trying to implicate Adam, and I don't think there's much chance you'll take such a risk."

Her uncle's face was ashen, and his step faltered as he turned and walked away from her. She knew from the defeated slump of his shoulders that he'd taken her threats at face value, but she felt no pride in having won this victory. She felt as dirty and cheap as the tactics she'd employed, and her stomach was churning with nausea, but she managed to maintain her scornful pose until Dennis had disappeared into the crowd.

For a long time after he'd gone, she remained immobile, oblivious to the rain and the cold and the people milling about. Then she saw Adam. He was several hundred yards away from her, helping two white-uniformed men load a stretcher into an ambulance. In spite of the smoke-misted distance between them she recorded the fact that it was Edwin Byrne who lay on the stretcher, and from that point her memories were chaotic.

She recalled racing toward Adam, crying his name as she ran, trying to make herself heard above the noise of the crowd. She remembered nearing the ambulance just as Adam climbed into it and crouched beside his father's inert form.

"Adam, wait!" she called. She had a stitch in her side and she was out of breath from running, so she slowed to a walk in order to catch her breath and call more loudly, "Please, Adam, wait for me!"

The attendant eyed her inquisitively. "Is she coming along?" he asked.

Without looking up, Adam replied curtly, "No. Let's just get my father to the hospital."

After an apologetic glance at Shannon the attendant followed Adam into the van, but she reached the ambulance in time to grab the handle and prevent the medic from closing the door.

"Why can't I go with you, Adam?" she entreated. "What's happened?"

Beneath the clear plastic of an oxygen mask Edwin Byrne's face was gray and pinched, and Adam was anxiously watching his father. It was the attendant who answered her last question, saying, "He's had a heart attack."

"Oh, God, Adam!" she cried. "I'm so sorry."

"Are you?" he asked. The coldness in his voice made her gasp.

"Of course I am! I'm your *wife*, Adam."

His eyes were inflamed and red-rimmed, and they were filled with condemnation when they met hers.

"That," he said grimly, "is a situation that's easily rectified." Turning to the attendant, he ordered harshly, "Let's go, damn it!"

She would never forget Adam's face at the moment when he wrenched the door from her clutching fingers and closed it between them. She wished her mind could erase the bitterness she'd seen there, wished she'd never seen the icy contempt in the dark eyes that only hours before had cherished and desired her.

She remembered her disbelief when the ambulance pulled away. She actually took a few running steps after it before she recognized the futility of trying to stop Adam from leaving her. Exhausted and shocked, she fell to her knees on the ground, and she had no idea how long she remained there, huddled and shivering in the rain, before Alice and Ned Penrose happened upon her.

"Come along, love," Alice cajoled. "This is no place for you. Let us take you home."

Later Alice told Agatha that at first Shannon had refused to leave the place where she'd last seen Adam, so even though he'd callously abandoned her, she hadn't yet given up hoping that eventually he would come back for her.

As she left the gazebo and started along the path toward the house, Shannon tried to recall when she had stopped hoping. She remembered that late in the afternoon on the day after the fire, Alice had brought a tray of food to her room. Dr. Follensbee had given her a sedative before she'd gone to bed and she still felt drugged, but she'd asked Alice if Chief Larkin's investigation had turned up anything conclusive.

"They haven't found a thing to support the arson theory," Alice replied. "I think they've decided to drop it."

"Do you think—" Shannon managed to choke back the

rest of the question, but the older woman answered as if she hadn't.

"I think it was the lightning that started the fire," said Alice in her no-nonsense way. "And I think, for a little while, Dennis's hatred of the Byrnes got the better of him. That's why he telephoned Adam and his father and asked them to come here last night. That's why he tried to fabricate evidence against Adam. I think, for a time, your uncle lost touch with reality, and he really *believed* the fire was Adam's doing."

Shannon was eager to subscribe to Alice's interpretation, and she nodded vigorously.

"Has Adam called?" she asked.

"He stopped by to pick up his medallion." Alice turned away and busied herself with rearranging the articles on the bureau and brushing imaginary dust from the gleaming cherry-wood surface. "He—uh—he left a message for you," she went on uneasily. "He asked me to tell you that his father would like to see you and he'd appreciate it if you'd visit him this evening."

"Mr. Byrne is in the hospital, isn't he?"

"Yes. His doctor is transferring him to the Mayo Clinic as soon as he's well enough to be moved. Adam said he might need open-heart surgery."

Through the partially open door that led to the bathroom, Alice spied the terry cloth robe. It lay in a muddy heap on the floor, but she scooped it up enthusiastically, exclaiming over its grimy condition. "I'd better see what I can do about these stains," she announced.

"No!" Shannon cried. "Leave it!" When the startled Alice had dropped the robe, she added in a conciliatory tone, "I prefer to take care of it myself."

"All right, Shannon, if you'd rather," Alice agreed. She

collected the untouched tray and marched briskly toward the hall.

"Didn't Adam leave any other messages for me?" Shannon asked hopefully. "Didn't he want to see me?"

Alice turned to look at Shannon, and her eyes were soft with compassion. "I'm sorry, love," she said gently, "but he didn't"

Shannon forced an overbright smile. "Maybe tonight, when I visit Mr. Byrne—"

"Yes, Shannon," Alice broke in. "Maybe tonight."

But Adam wasn't at the hospital that night, and Shannon's interview with Edwin Byrne was over in a matter of minutes.

"We're only letting you see him because he's been so upset about this," Edwin's nurse explained as she ushered Shannon to the cardiac-care unit. "His condition is extremely unstable and he's very weak, so try to keep it brief and, whatever happens, don't let him become agitated."

Shannon sat by Edwin's bedside and held his hand while he asked haltingly, "Has Adam told you anything about his mother?"

"Only a little," she replied.

"We've left our mark on him, his mother and I. He never had much of a family life. When he was a boy, I was preoccupied with my own growing pains and his mother wasn't around. Oh, she'd swoop down on us every other year or so and whisk Adam off to some Godforsaken place or other, and he really looked forward to his travels with her, but between visits she'd make well-intentioned promises and, inevitably, she'd break them. She's had several husbands and a succession of lovers, and the saddest part of it was that there were one or two of them that Adam developed a genuine fondness for before he learned that they weren't destined to be permanent fixtures in his life.

"And I wasn't any better as a father. When I saw what my mistrust of women was doing to Adam, I tried to make him understand that my experience with Nicole had soured my outlook and that all women aren't perfidious, but it was too late to undo the damage."

The effort of talking had tired Edwin, and he rested for a moment. When he continued, his voice was a little stronger. "Forgive me for asking," he said, "but I have to know. Was your uncle telling the truth last night, or do you really love my son?"

He studied her intently, and although the only answer she was capable of giving was a nod of her head, Edwin squeezed her hand and observed, "I can see that you love him, and I pray that you aren't easily discouraged."

Tears glistened on her lashes, and she responded in a quavering voice, "I try not to be."

"You're a very loving young woman, Shannon. My son needs you."

"And I need him."

"Then for his sake, and your own, don't give up on Adam. You've seen what's happened to your uncle and me because we haven't let bygones be bygones. I think you'll agree, it isn't very pretty. Don't permit yourself to be ruled by hatred. If you do, in the end it'll destroy you."

"I'll try not to," she promised soberly.

Consoled by her obvious sincerity, Edwin expelled his breath in a long sigh, relaxed against the pillows, and closed his eyes, dismissing her. He was peacefully asleep before she left the room.

In keeping with her promise to Adam's father, and

because she couldn't help herself, she'd continued to hope. It was foolish, for Adam didn't return her phone calls and he refused to see her. It was painful. She left herself open to fresh disappointments, to the hurt when she learned from Merry that Adam had left Galena to accompany his father to the clinic in Rochester, Minnesota. It was illogical, but she'd stubbornly looked for a ray of hope even in the brutal finality of that information.

"Rochester isn't far from Minneapolis," she remarked philosophically. "Maybe Adam will come and see me at the university."

"God!" Merry exclaimed. "You're hopeless!"

"No, Merry." Shannon smiled ironically as she contradicted her friend. "I only *wish* I were."

At Agatha's insistence she returned to college. She wrote to Adam at the Chicago address he'd given her, and her letters came back stamped "Addressee Unknown." She'd stopped writing, but she hadn't stopped hoping.

She went through the motions, apathetically pretending that nothing was changed. At the end of the fall semester her grades were so poor that she was put on probation and she spent Christmas at the campus, trying to catch up before classes resumed. The next semester she focused all her energies on her studies and she made the Dean's list.

That summer she found a temporary job in St. Paul. She couldn't bring herself to attend Merry and Gil's wedding.

She observed the first anniversary of her own wedding by removing her ring and storing it away at the back of her closet, in the box with the terry cloth robe. When fall came again, she registered for classes under her maiden name, but now and then she would take the box down and look at the ring, and whenever she caught a glimpse of a tall, dark-haired man, her heart did flip-flops before she recognized he wasn't Adam.

The following June, Merry and Gil visited Minneapolis. They invited Shannon to have dinner with them at their hotel one evening. Shannon dreaded seeing them, and she was relieved when neither of them mentioned Adam.

Merry was in the advanced stages of pregnancy. She was heavy and awkward, but she was radiant. During the evening there was one tense moment when Merry remarked, "It's funny how things have turned out. You wanted the marriage and kids bit and I'm the one who planned to stay single and have a career and play the field, but look at me now."

Smoothing over the tension, Shannon complimented her friend. "Motherhood seems to agree with you, Merry. You're positively blooming."

"I'm glad you put it that way, Shannon," said Gil. "Merry's getting fed up with people telling her how big she is."

"Can you blame me?" Merry asked testily. "It isn't as if I don't know perfectly well what a blimp I've turned into."

"But darling," Gil fondly teased, "you're such a cute little blimp! Anyway, when junior finally arrives, you might decide you prefer the disadvantages of pregnancy to two A.M. feedings, dirty diapers, and a steady diet of puréed carrots and peanut butter!"

Merry innocently widened her eyes at her husband. "Gilbert Rutherford!" she exclaimed. "Are you telling me that you're going to make *me* get up in the middle of the night? I thought that once your son or daughter was delivered, you'd take over."

Gil chuckled. "Sorry, doll, but it's not in the job description. If you'll think back to our wedding vows, you'll recall that at no time did I promise you that married life would be a bed of roses."

"And it's just as well it isn't," Shannon contributed. "It's a well-known fact that rose beds are chock-full of thorns and—er, steer manure."

Gil laughed at Shannon's hastily censored quip, but Merry was scandalized. "Why, Shannon!" she chided.

"Careful, Shannon," Gil interjected. "When Merry uses that tone, I know I'm in deep trouble."

"I'm as broad-minded as the next person," Merry defended herself, "but I can't help being shocked. I've never known Shannon to be indelicate."

When they parted company that night, Merry said, "You're different than you used to be, Shannon. Are you happy?"

"Happy?" Shannon tested the word as if it were completely foreign to her before she replied flippantly, "I don't ask for 'happy.' All I want is peace."

Even as she'd spoken, Shannon had realized how true this was. And she'd realized something else. At some time in the last few months she'd stopped seeing Adam in every stranger who resembled him, and she couldn't recall the last time she'd wept over her wedding ring.

Unnoticed, unmourned, without as much as a whimper, her hope had finally died. And, in a way, being without hope was even worse, for she had buried her dreams, and with them she'd buried a part of herself—perhaps the best part—but she hadn't stopped loving Adam. After that night she'd prayed for the day when she could truthfully say that her love for him was dead; but now, seven years after the fire, she was still waiting for that day.

CHAPTER SEVEN

Agatha was still awake when Shannon returned to the house. When Shannon passed her room on her way to bed, she called, "Come help me drink some of this cocoa. Alice always fixes enough for an army, so I had her bring an extra cup for you."

Smiling, Shannon accepted the invitation. She crossed the room and pulled a chair close to her grandmother's bedside. Her movements were unconsciously graceful as she sat down, for she was studying her grandmother.

Agatha's face was as pale as the linens on her bed. She was lying against a mound of pillows, and the massive pine headboard at her back emphasized her frailty. She seemed content to let Shannon serve the cocoa, and Shannon's heart contracted with grief at this evidence that her grandmother, who had always had vitality enough for ten women, now lacked the strength for even that easy task.

"Where have you been all evening?" asked Agatha.

"In the gazebo." Shannon passed the older woman her cup.

"It must be chilly out there tonight." Agatha hunched her shoulders and feigned a shiver. "Soon it will be too cold to use it."

"I thought I'd get a space heater. When the windows

are installed, that should be enough to keep it fairly comfortable, at least until winter sets in."

Agatha nodded and sipped some of her cocoa. "Merry telephoned. She wanted to ask you to have dinner with Gil and her tomorrow night."

Shannon glanced at her wristwatch. "I hadn't realized how late it is. I'll call her back in the morning."

"She sounded rather miffed because you haven't stopped by to see her since you've been home, so I took the liberty of accepting in your behalf."

"Thanks for the warning." Shannon smiled meaningfully. "How is Merry?"

"Matronly. Placid. Adam says—" Agatha caught herself uncomfortably in midsentence.

"It's all right, Gran." Shannon's tone was gentle, and she managed to maintain an unruffled expression. "What does Adam say?"

"He says Merry behaves as though she'd invented marriage. She's forever trying to play Cupid, and he's gotten very leery about accepting her invitations because he never knows who else she'll have at her house." Indignantly, Agatha added, "She even tried to fix him up with LuAnne Follensbee!"

"LuAnne!" Shannon shook her head perplexedly. "I never could figure out how a couple as nice as Dr. and Mrs. Follensbee could produce a daughter like LuAnne. But maybe she's changed."

"No," Agatha replied. "At heart LuAnne is still a frustrated burlesque queen."

Dumbfounded, Shannon stared at her grandmother. "I never realized you knew about LuAnne's exhibitionist tendencies!" she exclaimed.

"Oh, I've known about LuAnne all along." Agatha

102

nodded sagely. "Even when she was in kindergarten, her favorite subject was 'show and tell.' I suppose that's not so unusual," she added, "but most children grow out of that stage. LuAnne never did."

"How did you find out?" asked Shannon. "I certainly never told you."

"My dear Shannon," Agatha replied dryly, "when you have children, you pick up certain types of information by osmosis. With her first baby's birth certificate, each new mother is automatically issued an extra set of eyes for the back of her head!"

Shannon laughed merrily at the image this brought to mind, and Agatha smiled brightly at the infectious sound.

"Hearing you laugh does more for me than anything Dr. Follensbee could prescribe." She'd tried to keep her comment light and airy, but a note of tiredness had crept into her voice.

Shannon replaced her own cup on the tray and collected her grandmother's. "Would you like to go to sleep now?" she asked.

"No." Agatha answered without hesitation. "Stay with me awhile."

"Do you want me to read to you?"

"I'd prefer just to talk. If you'll look in the closet, you'll find a cardboard carton. There's something in it that I'd like to show you."

Shannon located the box and carried it to the bed. It was surprisingly heavy. Placing the box where it would be easily accessible to her grandmother, she asked, "What's all this?"

"My memories," Agatha replied softly. "The box had been down in the basement since the house was finished, but Alice came across it when she was doing her fall cleaning, and she thought I might like to sort through it."

Her grandmother didn't actually say 'one last time,' but a small voice inside Shannon's head included the phrase, and she watched through a mist of tears as Agatha opened the carton. With loving hands she removed scrapbooks, diaries, a stack of recipe cards bundled together with a rubber band, and a packet of love letters that had been written to her by Gavin. These were carefully secured with white satin ribbon.

"I'd like you to have these," Agatha said, her manner matter-of-fact. "When you've had the chance to read them, you can keep them or not, whichever you choose. But if you don't want them," she instructed, "I'd like them destroyed. I don't want some stranger handling them."

Putting the letters to one side, she took out a pair of incredibly tiny baby shoes and a jeweler's case containing a gold locket that folded out to reveal three locks of baby hair. Agatha indicated the fairest of the three. "This is yours," she said. She worked the hinge, opening a fourth compartment. This one was empty, and Agatha looked at it wistfully. "I had hoped to add a lock of my great-grandchild's hair before I died."

Painfully reminded of a time when she had hoped that she might be pregnant, Shannon cleared her throat. "Sorry I can't oblige you, Gran," she said huskily, "but it's customary for a girl to have a husband first."

"That's what I wanted to talk to you about," Agatha responded cryptically. She resumed sifting through her mementos and finally found what she was searching for. "Remember this?" she asked as she handed Shannon an ornately calfbound book.

104

"The family Bible?" Shannon murmured. "Of course I do."

Taking the book from Agatha's trembling fingers, she rested the weighty volume in her lap. It fell open naturally to the pages where the vital statistics of the MacLeods had been painstakingly recorded.

When she was a little girl, she'd whiled away many a rainy Saturday poring over these pages. Over the years the fine copperplate script of the earliest entries had faded until they were very nearly illegible, but it had given her a sense of continuity with the past to review the generations of MacLeod births, deaths, and marriages. And now, thanks to her, there would be an annulment to blot the spotless tradition of unbroken marriages.

She scanned the list swiftly, but when she came to the final entry, she saw that Agatha had recorded only her marriage to Adam. There was no mention of an annulment or divorce.

Perhaps it was an oversight. Although her grandmother was usually methodical to a fault about such things, she might have forgotten to update the records. Shannon stared at the entry for so long a time that the words began to swim and blur. Her eyes were widely dilated and stormy, full of pain and doubt, the only color in the whiteness of her face when she finally raised them to meet Agatha's. One look at her grandmother was all that was needed to answer the question that screamed through her mind. She got to her feet numbly, insensible that the Bible had slid to the floor.

"Adam and I decided that it would be easier for you to hear it from me," Agatha apologetically explained, "but I've put off telling you. He came by to see me tonight, and he made me realize how unfair I've been to you. He made

105

me see that I simply couldn't postpone it any longer. You have to know—"

"No," Shannon whispered. Her voice was fierce with denial and she shook her head, underscoring her rejection of the truth her grandmother was telling her. "It can't be—"

"Yes, Shannon, it's true," Agatha declared. "Legally you're still married to Adam."

Shannon's reaction was immediate and visceral. She did something she'd never, in all her twenty-five years, done before. She fainted.

It was the next day before she began to recover her equanimity. She told herself that once she'd had a beautiful dream, but she'd paid a terrible price for her vision of paradise when she'd awakened to the nightmare of loss and loneliness. For a long time she'd tried to ignore the truth, and this had only prolonged the ordeal. But she'd learned from her mistake, and *nothing* could induce her to repeat it.

This time she adopted a fatalistic attitude toward the inevitable outcome of her predicament.

Seven years ago—after the fire, after the lies Dennis had told—Adam had decided he no longer wanted her. He'd opted out of their marriage almost before it had begun. And nothing had changed. Adam hadn't wanted her then, he didn't want her now, and he never would. Doubtless he had his own reasons for not having had their marriage set aside. Probably she meant so little to him that he just hadn't gotten around to ending it.

Except for the day of her arrival she'd seen Adam only briefly. Whenever he'd visited Agatha, she'd excused herself and left them alone. And he hadn't tried to seek her out. Now she was resigned to the necessity of their meeting in order to work out a solution to their nebulous relationship.

At least she had been spared the humiliation of learning about their marital status from Adam. It would have been unbearable if he'd seen her volatile response to Agatha's revelation.

She wasn't in the mood for gaiety that night, and she prepared reluctantly to keep her engagement with Merry and Gil. To lift her spirits she wore a dress of fine lilac-colored velour. It brought out the amethyst flecks in her eyes and it had a swingy skirt that made her feel like dancing. Then, because her heart wasn't in the evening, she brushed her hair back from her smooth forehead more severely than ever and rolled it into the usual neat twist at the nape of her neck.

When they'd talked on the telephone, Merry had confessed that the invitation to her was an afterthought. She'd said she was inviting several couples, but she hadn't revealed that Adam would be among the guests, so Shannon was unprepared for his presence. Merry and Gil greeted her cordially at their front door, guided her into the living room, and suddenly, there he was—more attractive than any man had a right to be. He was wearing fawn slacks with a darker suede jacket, and her heart leaped into her throat at the sight of him.

Adam looked in her direction and the silvery chain of his medallion was visible in the open collar of his shirt. It caught the light and flashed its ominous warning. His clothes might be casual, but his eyes were intent and penetrating as they wandered over her face, and when they settled on the hollows at the base of her throat, she knew that he saw the pulses racing there. He nodded coolly before he turned attentively to the curvaceous blonde at his side and introduced her as Candy Carlson.

Shannon acknowledged the introduction smoothly enough, also the ones to a couple Merry identified as Jim and Lisa Gregory. "Jim was one of Adam and Gil's first clients when they opened their office," Merry said proudly.

Jim Gregory was a thickset, blue-jowled man and he seemed jovial enough, but his wife was a gimlet-eyed, sharp-voiced woman of thirty or so who regarded Shannon with unwarranted hostility, as if she suspected Shannon might make a play for her husband. Looking at the assembled guests, Shannon thought she knew how Davy Crockett must have felt when he'd found himself surrounded and hopelessly outgunned at the Alamo.

Walter Hensley, who was the final person at the dinner party, gravitated to her side. He touched her elbow and handed her a glass of wine, and Shannon was so relieved to see a friendly face that she smiled at him warmly.

"Remember me?" he asked.

Shannon nodded. "How could anyone forget the all-time greatest football hero Galena High ever produced?"

Walt grimaced wryly. "You'd be surprised how easy it is."

"What are you doing these days?"

"*Coaching* football at the high school, but if I don't come up with a winning season, I may not be there long enough for the ink on my contract to dry."

"Oh," Shannon responded inadequately, "I'm sorry."

"It's not your fault." Walt shrugged. "Who knows? Maybe I'll get lucky."

Casting about for a safer topic, Shannon hurriedly remarked, "I heard you'd married Marilyn Shields."

"We're separated," Walt replied shortly.

After this faux pas Shannon retreated to the relative security of silence. She smiled and tried to appear interested when spoken to, she answered questions that were intended for her, but she made no further effort to initiate conversation.

The evening limped along. Walt was morose, Lisa was watching her vigilantly and zealously guarding her husband, and Adam and Candy were pointedly ignoring her.

When they were getting into their coats prior to adjourning to the restaurant where the Rutherfords had made dinner reservations, Merry took Shannon to one side and tried to apologize.

"I swear I never meant for tonight to be like this," she murmured. "God, what a disaster! I've never known Lisa to be so bitchy. Jim's nice enough, but he's no special prize, so Lord only knows why she's acting as if he were the last man on earth. And as for Walt—well, my only excuse there is that he's been like a lost soul since Marilyn left, and I felt sorry for him. I thought the two of you might hit it off since you're both—"

Merry clapped her hands over her mouth and Shannon finished evenly, "Carrying a torch?"

"I can't believe I *said* that!" Merry exclaimed. "I'm not usually so tactless."

"Don't worry about it," Shannon comforted. "I'm not that fragile, and this seems to be the night for blunders. I am disappointed not to have met Tricia, though."

Merry brightened at the mention of her five-year-old daughter. "She *is* a darling. She's staying the night with my mother, but I promise you, we'll get together again soon."

Things did not improve during dinner, and by the time

the ill-assorted party trooped from the dining room to the taproom for after-dinner drinks, even Gil's hearty good-humor was strained. Shannon was tempted to forget about courtesy, bid the others good night, and make her escape.

It was only because she didn't want Adam to know how much it hurt her to see him with another woman that she slid quietly into the banquette. When it was too late to change her mind, she found herself trapped within the narrow confines of a booth intended for six but presently occupied by eight, sitting shoulder to shoulder between Adam and Walt. She tried to take up as little space as possible, and Adam leaned slightly forward, half turning toward Candy, but no amount of shifting about could diminish the pressure of his thigh against hers.

Adam was concentrating on Candy and seemed completely immune to Shannon's nearness. She, on the other hand, was increasingly uneasy, increasingly aware of the sensual touch of Adam's long, muscular thigh. When her drink was placed in front of her, she gulped it down. She tried to divert herself by listening to Lisa's monologue. It had something to do with the comparative merits of various day schools and her son's requirement for a completely unrestricted environment, and it went interminably, monotonously on.

At last Gil put an end to the lecture by asking Merry to dance, and when Lisa and Jim also left the table for the dance floor, Walt moved along the bench and Shannon quickly followed suit. This, she realized, was not much of an improvement, for although she'd ended the exquisite torture of the contact with Adam, in her new position she had an unobstructed view of Adam and Candy.

Candy Carlson was all of nineteen, Shannon decided. She was perky and cute, bouncy and bubbly, and she had all the exuberance of a cheerleader. She was also lousy with sex appeal and obviously turned on by Adam.

Even while Shannon was observing them, aware that her eyes were becoming glassy with envy, Candy was tilting her vivacious flower-face toward Adam as she proclaimed, "All *I* want from life is a husband and babies." The dramatic impact of her confession was lessened somewhat when she followed her announcement with a giggle and added, "At least *six* babies."

Candy gazed soulfully into Adam's eyes, and Shannon bit her tongue to keep from commenting that only a woman who already had five children could declare with any degree of credibility that she wanted six.

A steely edge hardened Candy's breathy, little-girl voice as she went on. "I think it's awful the way some women take motherhood so lightly. I want to raise my children so they'll feel it's their *duty* to make a really meaningful contribution to their fellowmen. That's why I'm going to set aside the next year and devote my time strictly to *defining* myself. Some people might think it's selfish, but I think it's essential to do that before I'll be able to be a really super mother."

"Good Lord, it's 'Supermom'!" Walt exclaimed in a droll undertone that only Shannon could hear. "I wouldn't have thought she'd need an entire year to 'define' herself." He shook his head uncertainly. "Five minutes maybe, but not a whole year."

Although Shannon covered her laughter with a cough, Candy sensed her amusement and turned round, delft-blue eyes on her.

"Adam tells me you're a teacher, Miss MacLeod, so I'm sure you can sympathize with my feelings about this." Even as she moved in for the kill, Candy smiled guilelessly

111

at Shannon. "I'll bet you're a very gifted teacher. A person as *mature* and *dignified* as you couldn't possibly have any problem enforcing discipline in the classroom."

Candy's thinly veiled insult was punctuated by her tinkling laugh. "I'm an idealist myself, you see, so I can't tell you how much I admire women who are *determined* enough to *insist* upon a career." Another adorable giggle. "And I especially admire the ones who remain true to their ideals." Giggle, giggle, "By the time they're *your* age, most women have sold out."

Shannon had made the error of trying to appear unfazed by Candy's attack by sipping her drink, and when Candy uttered her last pearl of wisdom, Shannon choked on it. While Walt was pounding her on the back, Adam put his glass down and pushed the table away from the bench.

"Candy," he directed smoothly, "let's dance."

"Oooh, Adam! I'd adore to!" Candy squealed with pleasure and bounced out of the booth. "Don't you think dancing is the most terrific exercise. I'm into aerobics and it's done wonders for my figure." Giggle, giggle. "Not that it was all that bad before!" Giggle, giggle. "It just sort of *lifted* everything and toned it and firmed it up. Honestly, Adam, I've never felt so *fit!*"

Candy thrust out her breasts and postured provocatively before she walked ahead of Adam toward the dance floor. She undulated as she walked, swinging her hips and giving him ample opportunity to judge for himself how uplifted and firm and fit she was.

Shannon's eyes were tearing, and she hoped Walt would attribute the tears to her coughing fit. She watched Candy cuddling into Adam's arms while they blended into the crowd of dancers, and watching them, she felt decrepit and old. She felt every bit as sexless and mature and dignified as the younger girl had described her.

"Candy *does* have a lovely figure," she said miserably.

"Shannon, my child," Walt replied, "even in bosoms there can be too much of a good thing. Especially when a lady's bust measures higher than her IQ. Candy's great-looking now, but she's the kind who's going to go to pot, and when she does, look out below!"

"She has a sparkling personality."

"That's true," Walt conceded. "I'll bet she even giggles in bed."

"She's so damned *young*!" Shannon lamented.

"You're not exactly over the hill yourself. At least, I hope you aren't, because I'm two years older than you, and you know where that would leave me."

Shannon shook her head glumly. "It's different for men."

"No, it isn't," Walt insisted. "Men worry about aging just as much as women do."

"But older men are still attractive to young girls."

"Which is great, if you happen to go for young girls. Mature women are much more sensuous. I'm fast becoming a wrinkle freak myself."

Shannon sighed. "The way I feel tonight, you've come to the right place!"

"Aw, come on, Shannon," Walt coaxed. "Don't let Candy's digs get to you. You'll be beautiful when you're eighty!"

"Thanks, Walt, but I don't think I can wait that long." New tears flooded her eyes and spilled over before she could stop them.

"Hey!" he exclaimed softly, covering her hand consolingly with his. "You're still in love with Adam, aren't you?"

Shannon nodded.

Walt frowned. "What's wrong with the guy, wasting time with Candy when he could have you?"

"He has his reasons." Shannon wiped away the tears with a cocktail napkin.

"Is he likely to change his mind?"

There was no need for Shannon to think about her answer to Walt's question. Her response was a husky, but unequivocal, "No."

"Well, then, how about coming out with me some night?"

This time Shannon didn't answer so quickly. "I'm not sure if that's a good idea," she said at last. "What about Marilyn? She might not understand—"

Walt's chin jutted out stubbornly. "Marilyn and I had a fight and she walked out. I won't try to kid you that I'm not still hung up on her, but I'm not looking for a consolation prize. If I were on the make, I'd try my luck with young Candy. I like you too much to do that to you. What I want is some female companionship. Hell, Shannon! All I really want is someone to *talk* to."

"About Marilyn and you?" Shannon asked gently.

"Partly," Walt admitted, "but I don't want a shoulder to cry on, either!" He paused to signal a passing cocktail waitress, holding up two fingers to order a second round of drinks. "I guess I'd like a woman's point of view, though," he continued absently. "It's been more than a month since Marilyn left, and I can't even remember what the big blowup was about. I thought she'd come to her senses by now. She's always been hot-tempered, but she's gotten over it long before this."

"Have you talked to Marilyn and let her know you want her to come back to you?"

"*She* started it! Why should I be the one to give in?"

"Because you love her," Shannon reasoned.

The waitress delivered their drinks just then, and she had to wait for Walt's reply until they'd been served. Even when the waitress had left, they kept their voices low and their heads close together, and they were intent on their conversation when Adam and Candy returned to the table. As soon as they arrived, however, Walt got to his feet and invited Candy to dance.

Left alone with Adam, Shannon concentrated on the music and the couples on the dance floor. She was uncomfortably aware of Adam studying her, and in what she hoped was a jaunty tone, she commented, "*Sandy* is a very good dancer, isn't she?"

"Yes, she is."

"Have you known her long?"

"Long enough," Adam replied tersely. "She's Lisa Gregory's kid sister, and Lisa, Jim, and I go way back."

They were silent for a time, and Shannon peered into her drink as if watching the ice melt were a matter of life-and-death importance to her.

"I talked to Agatha today," Adam remarked tonelessly. "She told me she'd finally gotten round to telling you we're still married."

Damn him for sounding so unconcerned, thought Shannon. "They say the wife is always the last to know," she managed to retort, "but in this case it's ridiculous."

Again they were silent, but now Shannon knew that Adam was irritated with her. He was giving extra careful consideration to his next approach, and she sensed it

115

would not be so amicable. Trying to land the first blow, she purred, "Does *Cindy* know you're married?"

"The young lady's name is *Candy*, and you damned well know it!"

"And you've developed a craving for sweets!" Shannon exclaimed tartly. Raising her glass to Adam, she toasted, "I'll drink to that," and downed her drink in one long swallow.

"That tears it," Adam muttered. With an abruptness that startled Shannon, he scraped the table back from the banquette and rose. Grabbing her wrist, he yanked her to her feet and towed her relentlessly behind him as he shouldered his way through the dancers and toward the rear exit of the cocktail lounge.

"What do you think you're doing?" Shannon protested.

"Stopping you from making a spectacle of yourself," Adam replied, grim-faced. "We have to talk, but a public barroom is hardly the place—"

"Talk?" she cried shrilly as he pushed her ahead of him through the door and allowed it to close after them. "What do *we* have to talk about?"

"Our marriage—"

"There's nothing to discuss," she said vehemently. "I assumed you'd tidied up that loose end years ago. I thought you'd had it annulled."

"Oh?" Adam drawled. "On what grounds?"

His eyes glowed like hot coals as he surveyed the indignant contours of her body, reminding her of the total abandon with which their marriage had been consummated. Shannon's cheeks stung and grew vivid with color.

"I'm relieved to see you're still capable of embarrassment," Adam said. "I take it that means you're not entirely without scruples." He smiled humorlessly. "Now, do

116

you want to hash this out here?" He glanced about, calling to her attention the fact that they were standing near the alley door of the supper club. Like common tavern brawlers they were surrounded by dingy brick walls and trash bins. "Or do you want to make it later?" he suggested. "After you've had a chance to cool down?"

Shannon leaned weakly against the wall, her head bowed in acquiescence. "Later," she mumbled diffidently.

Satisfied, Adam nodded and led the way inside.

CHAPTER EIGHT

The law offices of Byrne and Rutherford were on Prospect Street. They occupied the ground floor of one of the "Quality Hill" mansions that had been built by the mine owners in the early nineteenth century.

After stalling for several weeks, Shannon agreed to meet with Adam during his regular office hours in order to work out the details of their divorce. She thought this arrangement would make it easier to keep their discussion impersonal, and she admitted to herself that she would need all the help she could get to remain businesslike.

Even the way she dressed for her appointment with Adam was designed to remind her not to allow her emotions to rule her head—or at least not to show it. The teal-blue skirt with its matching jacket and the white silk blouse she chose to wear were as crisply tailored as those of the attractive middle-aged receptionist who greeted her and showed her into Adam's office.

"Mr. Byrne has been detained, but he should be here in fifteen minutes or so," the receptionist explained. "Would you like a cup of coffee or tea while you're waiting?"

"No, thank you," Shannon declined, pleased by the steadiness of her voice.

Smiling pleasantly, the receptionist returned to her

desk, and left to her own devices, Shannon assessed the room. She decided that Adam's office was not very conducive to formality. One wall was lined with books, but the others were paneled with silvery barnwood, and it was furnished with a classic mahogany table and a credenza instead of a desk. The Eames chairs and burgundy leather sofas projected masculine simplicity and comfort, while there were mullioned windows on either side of the room that contributed to its relaxed hominess.

From one window the view was of the smiling blue of October skies and towering maples raining saffron-yellow leaves upon the green hillside. From the window at the front of the house, Shannon could see downhill to the commercial district of Main Street with its huge metal flood gates at one end, and beyond Main Street to the old Market House and the dike that, with the floodgates, helped protect the downtown area from inundation.

The shallow trickle that was the Galena River shone like pewter in the afternoon sun. As it snaked past the town the stream was so diminished by deposits of silt that it was hard to believe there had once been a busy port just below Commerce Street. It was harder still to believe that the peaceful little community had once been a thriving metropolis.

Back in the 1830s, because of the lead mines and its fine harbor, Galena had been the most important city in Illinois—far more important than upstart Chicago. But all the hustle and bustle of those days was just a memory now, and the town itself was like a historical display in a museum; a sort of life-size diorama.

The locals called Galena "the town that time forgot." They took a perverse pride in its immutable character. They liked to recount how Ulysses Grant had left for his presidential inauguration with the admonition "Don't change anything till I return." Then, so the story went, the general never came back to live in Galena, and the town hadn't changed.

Sheltered by hills so steep that stairways were necessary for pedestrians to climb them, Galena nestled sleepily into the narrow valley beside its vanishing river and became an antiquarian's delight. It was an enchanted Rip Van Winkle of a town whose slumber was disturbed only by the seasonal migration of tourists.

Some of the visitors fell under the spell of Galena and stayed, some of the younger Galenians left for greener pastures. The dike was added, and the floodgates. Some of the vintage buildings were restored, a few new buildings were constructed. But at heart the town remained unaltered, no matter how great the changes in the outside world.

Shannon was still at the window when Adam's Mercedes came into view and turned into the driveway at the far end of the house. She watched, her throat aching with unshed tears, while Adam climbed out of the car. A roguish grin flashed across his face as he waved to an elderly neighbor who was preparing his garden for the coming winter. He paused to exchange pleasantries with the neighbor, his back to the window.

Adam's knees were slightly bent and his narrow hips were resting against the fender of the car, and she drank in the sight of him as if she were a sponge soaking up water. And as if admiring Adam were precisely what nature had created her for, she was unable to tear her eyes away from his wide shoulders and the glossy, raven-dark back of his head until he glanced toward the window of his office.

He seemed to be looking directly at her, and she ducked away from the window. Her heart hammered rapidly beneath her breastbone when her sudden movement allowed the openweave drapery to fall back into place.

Had Adam seen her? she wondered. The last thing she wanted was for him to know how deeply she still loved him.

She ran to the bookcase, hurriedly made a selection, and darted to a sofa. Holding the open book in her lap, she stared at it blindly, hoping it would appear to Adam that she'd been unconcernedly passing the time by reading while she waited for him.

A few more minutes went by before Shannon heard Adam's voice in the hallway. "Oh, Doris," he called to the receptionist, "when you have a moment, would you call Stan Richmond to confirm our appointment for this evening. And don't put any calls through until my wife has left."

Fleetingly, Shannon wondered why he had referred to her as his wife, then the door opened, Adam entered the room, and she gripped the edges of the book tightly to keep her shaking hands from revealing her inner turmoil. She watched him through her lashes, studying him obliquely while he deposited his attaché case on the worktable and leafed through his messages. Finally he gathered up the memos, stuck them beneath the edge of the blotter, and looked at her. The corners of his mouth tilted into a smile when he saw what she was reading.

"That's remarkable," he said in a dry, satirical tone. "I had no idea you were so interested in *Illinois Statutes.* You're the first person I've ever known who could read that particular book upside down. Volume II maybe, but not volume III."

Shannon started and guiltily righted the book. Her cheeks flushed hotly before she could regain her aplomb.

"I'm sorry I kept you waiting," Adam went on. "Dad flew in from California this morning, and his plane was late."

"That's all right." Still striving for nonchalance, Shannon shrugged. "How is your father?"

"Very well, thanks. He's looking forward to seeing you," Adam replied crisply. "Now, shall we skip the rest of the small talk and get to the point of our meeting?"

"I'd like nothing better," Shannon stiffly agreed, "but I really don't understand what there is to talk about. It goes without saying that I won't contest any action you file, and since there's no question of any sort of settlement, I can't see why obtaining a divorce should present any problem."

"The 'problem' is that there seems to be a communications gap." Adam paced restlessly around to the front of the table, continuing to approach her until he loomed over her so forbiddingly that she felt even more distinctly at a disadvantage. "You see, Shannon," he said without inflection, "I don't want to talk about divorce. I want to discuss our marriage. I'd like for us to make another try at it."

"That's impossible!" Shannon cried. Thinking only of escape, she jumped to her feet and started toward the door.

"Not at all," Adam calmly returned. "It wasn't impossible seven years ago and it isn't now."

Shannon wheeled around to confront him, feeling safer with the width of the room dividing them.

"When you first came home, you told me that there was no one special waiting for you in Minneapolis." His eyes narrowed as he searched her face. "But Agatha tells me

122

you've been seeing Walt Hensley lately. If you're making it with him and you're afraid he might object, I can assure you, he won't. He's still in love with his wife."

"You can't honestly think I don't know that." Rankled by his careless assumption that she and Walt were having an affair, she glared at Adam combatively. "You don't deserve an explanation, but I'll give you one because you've made allegations that could damage the reputation of a very good friend. The truth is that *I'm* the one who convinced Walt to swallow his pride and make the first move. He and Marilyn have reconciled, and not only am I aware that he loves her, I'm happy for them!"

"In that case, what have you got to lose?" Adam argued. "The least you should do is hear me out. If you'll try to remain objective, you might even decide that the suggestion isn't as offensive to you as it appears."

What troubled Shannon was that she *wasn't* offended by the idea of giving their marriage another chance. In fact, she was tempted by it. There was nothing she had ever wanted even a fraction as much as she wanted to be a real wife to Adam. But having once found her way back from the abyss of despair into which she'd plunged when she'd seen her marriage broken, she knew, with a conviction so strong that she felt it to the marrow of her bones, that she could not survive losing Adam a second time.

Shaking her head dubiously, she asked, "Why now, Adam, after all these years?"

"There are any number of reasons," he answered steadily. "For openers there are your grandmother and my father. Nothing would please them more than seeing us back together. Secondly, we're older and wiser now, and each of us is well acquainted with the other's shortcomings, so we know what we're getting into. And we're past the age where we think we require romance to be happy.

"Before I mislead you, though, I want to say up front that I'd expect you to fulfill all of the usual wifely duties, in and out of bed. I don't foresee any difficulties in that area," he added sardonically, "because we already know that we're sexually compatible, and I still believe I was right about you when I told you that you're the kind who won't be satisfied with anything less than the whole ball of wax—and that includes babies."

"That has to be the most calculating, cold-blooded line of reasoning I've ever heard!" Shannon exclaimed.

She had listened to Adam's calm summation with a growing sense of unreality. Maybe he didn't need romance, but when she'd heard him speak of it so dismissively, she'd discovered that she did. She'd realized she still needed sentiment and tenderness as well. But most of all she needed love.

"What about *love*, Adam?" she asked softly. "What about passion? What about *any* feelings? Do emotions have a role in your future, or are they too apt to mess up your carefully laid plans—" Shannon trailed into silence when she saw that she had gone too far and that her taunts had angered Adam.

His mouth was white-rimmed, compressed to a grim line, and although she wanted to run from his office, she was riveted by the predatory glitter in his eyes as he closed the distance between them with a few long strides. In the next instant his arms were around her, effortlessly overcoming her frantic resistance to their savage strength, while his hands curved over the gentle swell of her buttocks to pull her even closer, crushing her softness against his unyielding masculine hardness.

When her struggles were subdued, one of his hands followed the length of her spine, from the small of her back to the nape of her neck. He raked his fingers through her hair, careless of whether or not he hurt her, scattering the pins that secured it and sending them flying. Tears sprang to her eyes as he loosened her hair, and when it lay in wild disarray about her shoulders, he grasped a handful of it to force her head back and prevent her from turning her face away from him.

"You haven't changed as much as I thought." His hands gentled when he saw her tears, and the velvety timbre of his voice was intimate and seductive. "If my approach has been too analytical for your tastes, you have only yourself to blame. From your appearance and the way you've been eluding me, I thought you might prefer a rational appeal to a sexual one, but if it's passion you want, I'm more than willing to oblige."

Slowly, deliberately, as if he had all the time in the world, he touched his mouth to hers, brushing his lips back and forth playfully, molding his mouth to hers with the lightest possible pressure until Shannon was conscious only of the erotic teasing of his lips. Her breath sighed through her own parted lips as she surrendered to the soft invasion of his tongue, and long before Adam ended the kiss, she was utterly devastated.

She swayed submissively against him, drugged by his sensuous exploration of her mouth and so weak with longing that her knees were incapable of supporting her. Her hands fluttered uselessly against his chest, and she clutched at the lapels of his jacket to steady herself.

"Please," she whimpered.

"Please what, Shannon? Please make love to you, or please don't?

"Please *don't.*"

He bent his head, burying his face in the hollow of her neck and holding her so tightly in his arms that she felt the shock wave of desire that shuddered through him as acutely as she felt the instinctive response of her own body.

"Why not?" he whispered thickly. "You want it as much as I do. You always did. You've always been a lusty little thing, and we were incredibly good together. Was it ever as good with any of the other men you've known?"

"No—" Her cry was muffled and indecisive, for he was caressing her persuasively, compellingly, and despite the barrier of her clothing the touch of his hands was incendiary. Even to her own ears the protest sounded false.

He raised his head to look down at her, and his laughter rang out bitterly when she closed her eyes to shut out the sight of the harsh derision in his.

"Why try to deny it?" he drawled insolently. "You may be guilty of many things, but you've never been hypocritical about sex, and it must give you some satisfaction to know how much I want you." His hands spanned her waist so that his fingertips dug painfully into her back and her eyes flew open. "Tell me, Shannon," he demanded, "how many men have you made fools of with your innocent eyes and your sweet siren's body?"

"I've never—"

His hands tightened punishingly. "How many, damn it!"

"Dozens and dozens! So many, I lost track!" Goaded by his insulting treatment into lashing out at him, she nearly screamed the lie.

No sooner were the words out than Shannon wished she could retract them. For one unguarded moment Adam's hard mask of indifference slipped and the expression in his eyes was defenseless and so full of anguish it was as if some inner light had been extinguished, leaving him groping in the dark. She felt she had glimpsed, through a chink in his armor, his own private hell.

She wondered later if she might have imagined it, because he recovered so quickly, thrusting her away from him and turning on his heel to walk away from her. His back was to her as he stood at the window, but his clenched fists and the rigid set of his shoulders revealed his outrage.

"If that many men have had you," he said flatly, "one more won't matter. The only difference is that this time, instead of giving your all for dear old Dennis, you can square it with your conscience by telling yourself you're going to bed with me for *auld lang syne,* or for science, or that you're striking another blow for the sexual revolution. You could say that you owe it to Agatha, or to yourself. You might even say that you owe it to me. Come to think of it"—he laughed again, mirthlessly, abrasively—"I could establish a powerful case for that last excuse."

"P-please don't," she implored him brokenly, trying to propitiate his icy fury. "There haven't been any others, Adam. Only you."

Perhaps the note of repentance in her voice convinced him that this was the truth, or it might have been the fact that when he turned to look at her, she met his eyes squarely. For what seemed an eternity he held her gaze. His study of her was so piercing that she felt he had laid bare her very soul, but she withstood his mute interrogation without flinching, and finally Adam nodded and turned to the windows once again.

"I think we understand each other," he said gruffly.

"I'd like you to at least consider my proposition before you give me your answer. Think it over. Feel free to discuss it with your grandmother or with anyone else whose opinion you value."

Shannon hadn't intended to make even the smallest concession. She had planned to politely decline Adam's proposal and put the whole issue of their marriage firmly behind her, and her voice was high-pitched with surprise as she heard herself promise, "I'll do that."

CHAPTER NINE

Gil Rutherford's forehead was furrowed with concern as he stood at the kitchen window, looking out at his daughter. With careful, mincing steps Tricia was walking down the sidewalk at the back of their house. Although the five-year-old was so absorbed in maintaining her pose of adult decorum that the tip of her tongue was poking busily from one corner of her mouth, she tripped occasionally over her trailing skirt or because of the oversize high-heeled shoes she was wearing. Her impish little face was garishly made up, and she sparkled with an assortment of bangles and beads that she'd confiscated from Merry's collection of costume jewelry.

"Are you *sure* Tricia will be all right on her own?" Gil asked fretfully.

"She'll hardly be alone, Gil." Merry smiled indulgently at her husband. "She's meeting several of her friends, and Gail Sommers is going along to keep an eye on all of them."

"But Gail's only thirteen." Gil sounded more worried than before.

"She's a very responsible thirteen," Merry pointed out, "and she's had loads of experience with little ones. After all, she's the oldest of six children."

"I don't know, Merry." Gil shook his head. "Maybe I should go with them just to be on the safe side."

"If you do, Tricia will never forgive you. She's been counting on going trick-or-treating with her friends, without her parents tagging along to cramp her style. Anyway, it's broad daylight and they're staying in the neighborhood." Merry wrinkled her nose derisively. "It's a far cry from when we were kids and got to go out at night on Halloween."

"And play tricks and forget about the treats," Gil suggested.

"Maybe *you* did, but I was always very well behaved."

Even Merry's saucy retort failed to distract Gil, and he complained, "Tricia's gotten to be so grown up since she started kindergarten."

"She's five years old, honey," Merry reminded him. "She's not a baby any longer."

"Don't I know it!" he exclaimed. "Who—or what—is she supposed to be in that getup?"

"I'm not sure," Merry admitted. "She figured out the costume all by herself. I'm afraid it may be her idea of what a 'mommy' looks like."

Gil sighed. "It's sad to see her growing up so fast."

"It'll be a while yet before she's ready to leave home for good," Merry said dryly. "Since you miss having a baby around so much, maybe it's time we had another one."

"Aha! I've got you now, my proud beauty!" Glancing over his shoulder, Gil grinned and winked at Shannon, who was sitting at the kitchen table. "There's a witness present, so I just might hold you to that."

"Oh, you—If that's not just like a lawyer!" Laughing helplessly, Merry gave her husband a playful shove toward the door. "Go on, you'll be late for your round of golf."

When Gil had left for the country club, commenting dolefully that he knew when he wasn't wanted, Merry refilled Shannon's coffee cup and poured out more for herself before she rejoined Shannon at the table.

"Now, where were we?" she asked.

"I believe I was telling you how adorable Tricia is," Shannon replied.

"She did look awfully cute in her costume," Merry agreed, "but that's not what we were talking about. As I recall, I was about to give you some invaluable advice about Adam."

"Merry, I'm not sure—"

"Well, *I* am," Merry broke in. "In my opinion you'd be an idiot to turn him down, and for the life of me I can't see why you're hesitating. I saw the way you were watching him with Candy the other night. You were like a starving kid looking in the bakery window! Furthermore, if you didn't want to go back to him, you wouldn't have needed to consult anyone. You'd have said 'Thanks, but no thanks' and gone on your way."

"It isn't as simple as that."

"Oh, isn't it?" Merry arched an eyebrow at Shannon in inquiry. Then, answering her own question, she said, "No, I suppose it isn't that straightforward. No doubt you've complicated the issue by dragging in all sorts of extraneous garbage that has no bearing at all on what's really at stake. If you ask me—"

"I wasn't aware that I had," Shannon interposed.

"If you *don't* ask me," Merry qualified, "I'll tell you anyway, that this is strictly between you and Adam. He must want you or he wouldn't have asked you to come

131

back to him. And either you want him or you're doing a damned good imitation of a lady who's pining away for love. Have you taken a good look at yourself in a mirror lately?"

Although she knew she had lost weight and that she was pale and listless, Shannon shook her head. She hadn't had a full night's sleep since her meeting with Adam, but for all her soul-searching and its accompanying toll of sleepless nights, she was no closer to a decision than she'd been at the beginning. Her heart tugged her in one direction, while her mind pulled her just as strongly in another, until she felt she was being torn apart by the choice she must make.

It didn't help matters that her uncle and her grandmother offered such contradictory advice. Agatha was wholeheartedly in favor of her reconciliation with Adam, while Dennis was adamantly opposed, and neither of them missed any opportunity to express their opinions on the subject. Shannon appreciated their concern, but all of this only added to her confusion.

Even Alice and Ned Penrose had gotten into the act. "You love him, Shannon," said Alice. "That's the bottom line." Ned chose to play it safe by offering the all-occasion nostrum, "It's time to fish or cut bait."

Everyone seemed quite capable of defining her feelings for Adam, but she didn't need anyone to tell her that she loved him, and she hadn't needed Merry to tell her that Adam wanted her, because she already knew that he did. The virile thrust of his body against hers when he'd held her in his arms that day in his office had made that clear.

From remarks he'd let fall it was apparent that Adam still believed she had betrayed him seven years ago. In the light of that, what she needed to know was whether he could ever care for her at all.

Instead of going directly home when she left Merry's house on that Halloween afternoon, Shannon drove impulsively on to Eagles Nest. She didn't go inside. For some reason the thought of being shut in by four walls and a roof, even in a room as large as the lobby of the lodge, made her feel claustrophobic, so she followed the walkway that led to a terrace overlooking the Mississippi.

The airport limousine was drawn up at the main entrance, but she was relieved to find the terrace deserted. Choosing a bench that was some distance away from the building, she sat down.

The wooded bluffs on the far side of the river were tinted amber and russet by the palette of the waning season, and for half an hour or more she let the tranquillity of this view work its magic on her frayed nerves. Only when she felt calmer did she turn to look at the imposing half-timbered edifice of the chalet.

From the many improvements she'd noticed about the grounds, it was easy to see that Eagles Nest had prospered in the years since Shagbark's closing, but in spite of its old-world charm and the glowing colors of its rosy brick and resplendent white stucco, the building had an oddly sullen, closed-in appearance. Its windows reflected the crimson of the setting sun and were rendered opaque, making it seem oddly scornful of the natural beauties outside its walls.

Shivering, whether because of this notion or from the chill in the air now that the sun had gone down, Shannon looked away from the lodge in time to see a tall silver-haired man making his way up the trail from the river.

When the hiker was near enough that she could see his features more clearly, she recognized him as Edwin Byrne.

She hadn't seen Edwin since she'd visited him in the hospital after he'd had his heart attack, but from the youthful spring in his step and the ease with which he covered the steep incline, it was apparent that he'd made a full recovery. He was heading toward the rear entrance to the lobby, but at the last moment he spotted Shannon and changed course.

"This is an unexpected pleasure," he called as he approached the bench. "Are you looking for Adam?"

"No, I—" Shannon got uncertainly to her feet. "Actually, I'm not sure why I'm here. I was on my way home from the Rutherfords', and I guess I just didn't feel up to dealing with my family."

"If you've been at the Rutherfords', then you must know Adam is golfing with Gil," Edwin divulged. "He didn't say what time to expect him home, but his loss is my gain. Or it will be, if I can talk you into having dinner with me."

He smiled gallantly at Shannon, and for the first time she saw the strong resemblance between Edwin and his son. Seeing Edwin smile was like gazing thirty years into the future and seeing in his father's lean, intelligent face the way Adam would look when his hard features had been gentled by time.

"I'd like that," she slowly replied, astonished to discover that she meant it. "But they'll be expecting me at Shagbark."

"You can call from my apartment and let them know where you are."

Shannon glanced deprecatingly at her camel corduroy slacks, hooded sweater, and knee boots. Because she'd been helping out at the Halloween party at Tricia's school earlier in the day, she'd dressed accordingly. Although her clothing was warm and practical for a children's party, it was hardly suitable for dining out.

"I'd like very much to have dinner with you," she said, "if you don't mind my scruffy appearance."

"Nonsense!" Edwin exclaimed. "You look charming."

He took her arm as they crossed the uneven flagstones of the terrace. When they reached the lobby door, he held it for her to precede him, and paused just outside to fill his lungs with the tangy evening air.

"I must say it's good to be home," he remarked. "San Francisco is a delightful city and the West Coast climate is certainly agreeable, but I missed the change of seasons and my daily walk beside the river." He pointed toward a grove of trees at the edge of the bluff. "Do you see that snag just there?"

Shannon sighted along his extended arm, nodding when she saw the gaunt branches of a dead elm starkly etched against the pale apricot of the western sky.

"And can you see the nest at the top?" Edwin asked.

Because it was so large it was clearly visible, and again Shannon nodded.

"That's the eyrie," he said. "Until about 1960 a pair of bald eagles lived there year-round."

Her eyes widened with interest. "I thought eagles migrated south for the winter."

Edwin shook his head. "Not always. There was enough open water hereabouts for this pair to feed through the winter. When Adam was a boy, he used to spend hours watching them and their offspring. For months he saved all his spending money, and he used it to buy a pair of binoculars and build an observation platform so he could get a better view of the birds."

Shannon's surprise that Adam, who was always vitally in motion, could be so patient for anything other than fishing must have shown in her face, because Edwin boasted, "My son has unusual powers of concentration, and once his interest is stimulated he can be extremely persevering. After the birds had abandoned the eyrie, he even climbed up to the nest. That's where he found the medallion he wears. He collected quite a few other trinkets from it as well. You must ask him to show them to you sometime."

Shannon stirred uneasily. Adam had never told her where he'd gotten the ankh. "Whatever happened to the eagles?" she asked.

"They were very old—too old to breed, although they still went through the courting rituals of strengthening the eyrie. Then one November morning the male eagle flew off and never returned to the nesting tree. We never found out what happened to him, but we assumed that some stupid fool shot him.

"The female stayed in the vicinity for a while; perhaps two weeks or so. We'd see her in another tree that had been one of their favorite perches. She hardly moved from it, and now and again she'd give her shrill cry. In a way it was uncanny. It was as if she were sending up some kind of guiding signal to her mate. From her behavior it was evident she was mourning him. Occasionally she'd find a dead fish on the riverbank, but she didn't even leave the perch to hunt for food. Finally she just left."

Shannon swallowed hard in an effort to clear the lump of tears in her throat, and still unsure of her voice, she touched Edwin's hand sympathetically.

"I'm sorry, my dear," Edwin apologized, exerting himself to produce a smile and patting the hand she'd laid on his. "I shouldn't have begun our evening on such a sorrowful note."

"It's all right," she replied. "It is a sad story, but it's a fascinating one as well. Not only about the eagles but about Adam. He's never told me very much about himself." Somewhat shakily she returned Edwin's smile. "To tell you the truth," she said, "I'm surprised that he's contented to practice law in a town as quiet as Galena."

"Oh, but Adam is a political activist, too," Edwin returned. "He serves on the Natural Resources Board and he's very involved with the Wildlife Preservation League. Besides which, he still manages to go adventuring for a time every winter. Last year it was a dig on the Yucatán Peninsula, and the year before it was a treasure hunt in the Florida Keys. So you see, he still has his vagabond shoes!"

Edwin's smile twisted ruefully. "Unfortunately, even I don't know my son very well. We've been closer companions since my heart attack, and I'm thankful for that, but I still regret my earlier failures as a parent."

"Adam is terribly protective of his independence," Shannon commented softly.

"I know," Edwin replied, "and that degree of autonomy can be terribly lonely. He needs you, Shannon, and he loves you. He may not be aware of it himself, but I'm as certain of that as I am that there will be a sunrise tomorrow."

Shannon was so encouraged by Edwin's assertion that she neglected to ask him why he was so sure of Adam's feelings for her. She was so buoyed by his confidence that she felt as if she were walking on air as she followed him across the lobby.

137

Because it was the off-season there were only a few people about. The desk clerk was leafing through a magazine, but when they stopped at the registration desk, he glanced up and smiled.

"It's quiet tonight, Frank," Edwin observed.

"Sure is," the clerk agreed. "There aren't even any messages for you, Mr. Byrne."

He inclined his head toward the bank of mailboxes at his back to emphasize their emptiness, and Edwin shrugged and turned away from the desk, continuing past the elevators to the broad, branching stairway. As they climbed, Shannon trailed one hand along the satiny finish of the banister, appreciative of its lustrous patina and handsomely carved detail.

"I hope you don't mind walking up to my apartment," Edwin said. "It's part of the regimen for my heart to avoid using elevators whenever possible."

"Of course not," Shannon quickly denied. "It's only two flights and I can use the exercise." Before they reached the first landing, she was panting a bit from trying to keep up with his strenuous pace. "Besides," she admitted wryly, "I seem to be out of condition myself."

"During the winter I try to climb the stairs backward at least once a day," Edwin confided. "It looks a little strange, but it's really quite a good way to keep in shape for skiing."

Shannon laughed. "Now I know where Adam gets his endless store of energy."

"Why, thank you, my dear." Edwin's smile revealed how pleased he was by this comparison.

He unlocked his apartment, and she stood just inside the doorway to the living room, admiring its warmth and coziness, while he moved about turning on lamps and drawing the drapes against the darkness outside.

"As you can see," Edwin remarked, "except that it's a little shabbier than the last time you were here, nothing has changed. Once things are arranged to my liking, I prefer to leave well enough alone."

He looked forlornly about him. "That was one of the things Nicole and I used to argue about. She was an inveterate furniture mover. She was forever trying things this way and that and shuffling in new pieces. I was never sure what I'd find when I came home. She accused me of being stodgy, but frankly I found it unsettling."

"I can understand why you would," Shannon murmured.

"Can you really?" Edwin asked wistfully.

Nodding thoughtfully, she said, "I suppose having a low tolerance for the pace of city life is one of the hazards of growing up in a town like Galena, but when I moved to Minneapolis, one of the hardest things to adjust to was the rate of change.

"In my neighborhood there are very few landmarks. It seems as if the minute construction on a building is finished, it's put up for sale, or remodeled, or torn down. And it's not only the physical environment that seems transitory, but the people! Friends move away and strangers take their place, and no sooner do they become your friends than they leave too—or you do—and the cycle begins all over again. So it isn't at all surprising if a person needs some kind of refuge from the rat race."

"I couldn't have put it better myself!" Edwin beamed at her. "You're truly *simpático,* young Shannon." Sobering, he chided himself, "But I'm forgetting my duties as your host. If you'd like to, you can telephone your grandmother

139

from the extension in the bedroom. It's through the door at the end of the hall."

Touched by his obvious desire to win her approval, grateful that she had been able to return the favor by lifting his spirits as, only a few minutes before, he'd bolstered hers, Shannon left the living room to make her phone call.

CHAPTER TEN

Agatha MacLeod died on a stormy night in mid-November. She seemed almost to welcome death, and she died with dignity and with merciful swiftness.

When George Follensbee had diagnosed her illness, she'd asked him not to take any drastic measures that would serve only to prolong death. "I've had a long and productive life," she'd told him, "and for the most part it's been a happy one. God knows I'm afraid of dying, but I'm even more frightened of doing it badly. When my time is up, I don't want to linger." She'd smiled gamely at him. "I've always had an excellent sense of timing, and I don't want to spoil my record."

The doctor respected her wishes, and she died peacefully, surrounded by friends and loved ones, knowing that her granddaughter's future was assured.

In the end she had only to see Shannon and Adam as they sat close together at her bedside to recognize that their reunion was inevitable. "You're going back to your husband," she said to Shannon. As she made this forecast Agatha's voice quavered and was nearly inaudible, but her eyes were clear.

Shannon looked quickly from her grandmother to Adam. His face was haggard with fatigue, but he met her gaze steadily, and in that moment she acknowledged how deeply she loved him and how inextricably their lives were bound.

"Yes," she replied, awed that her grandmother could have been aware of her decision before she'd made it.

"That's good." Agatha closed her eyes wearily. "I've been waiting for you to come to your senses and admit that you have no other choice." Her eyes opened and focused sharply on Adam. "She has no other choice, has she, Adam?"

"No," he affirmed. "And neither have I."

Agatha's conscience was appeased. She was content that their reconciliation would atone for the lies she'd told, and in the last minutes of lucidity before she lapsed into a coma, it was she who tried to reassure Shannon. "It will all work out," she predicted serenely. "You'll see."

Dennis was seated at the other side of the bed, holding his mother's hand and crying. He was trying to muffle his sobs with one hand over his face, but his shoulders shook with paroxysms of weeping.

"Look at me, son." Agatha gently touched his cheek. As if to infuse Dennis with her strength, she prompted, "Remember our bargain."

Dennis nodded. "No sad songs," he recited. Still fighting to regain his composure, he smiled tearfully at his mother as he pledged, "But I'll plant roses round your head and a hickory tree at your feet."

Agatha was struggling to draw each tortured breath, and her eyes were suddenly vacant. "I'm like the hickories," she murmured, barely moving her lips. "Tough—and resilient—" She closed her eyes for the last time, and her hand fell limply away from Dennis's cheek, plucked at the counterpane a few times, and was still.

142

Through a blur of tears Shannon saw how tiny her grandmother had become. *How fragile she looks,* Shannon thought, *and how tranquil.* "And *beautiful,*" she amended aloud, her voice breaking on the words. "The most beautiful lady I'll *ever* know."

"And beautiful," Dennis echoed.

Her uncle's voice sounded hollow and faraway, as if it were receding, and Shannon blindly reached for Adam. He caught her close, and she wrapped her arms around his neck, chokingly tight, as if she were panicking, drowning, while he held her so tightly it was painful.

"It's all right, baby," he whispered. "It's all right." The tears he would have shed were a frozen lake inside him, and he remained dry-eyed as he and Shannon held and rocked one another, striving together to surmount grief; but Shannon's tears were soft and warm against his cheek, a soothing balm that comforted him.

It seemed natural to Shannon to turn to Adam for comfort after her grandmother's death. It seemed right to cry out her grief in his arms. Until the funeral was over, she moved through the days like an automaton, but she kept busy. When a week had gone by, because of Adam's kindness and with the support of Alice and Ned, she began to recover from her apathy.

On the Friday after Thanksgiving, Gil and Adam stopped by for the reading of the will, and despite her grief, Shannon was shocked by the manner in which her grandmother had distributed her estate. She was dismayed to learn that Agatha had left the lion's share of the Mac-Leod acreage to Adam and her jointly, stipulating that it was to be held in trust for their children. And that was not all. The land was further entailed. If their marriage was

childless, if they were divorced, or if she were to prede-
cease Adam, the undivided interest in the land was to
revert to him.

There were generous cash bequests for Alice and Ned
and some minor contributions to charity, but to Dennis,
Agatha had bequeathed only the house and the few acres
of ground around it.

Although Shannon wanted to rail at the injustice of the
will, she forced herself to listen quietly until Gil had
finished reading. While his voice droned on, she studied
the faces of the others in the room, looking for some clue
that they were as surprised as she was that Agatha had
denied Dennis the inheritance that was rightfully his.

She could see Adam only in profile and his face was
impassive, but there was a tense, expectant quality in the
way he sat so still.

Alice was weeping softly into her handkerchief and Ned
was patting her on the shoulder, while Dennis was
slumped drunkenly in his chair with his unshaven chin on
his chest. Occasionally he splashed more bourbon into his
glass from the bottle at his elbow, but except for this he
didn't move.

Was it possible that the conditions of his mother's will
hadn't penetrated his whiskeyed haze? Shannon wondered
bleakly, or was she the only one who'd found the will
totally unexpected? She was so confused that her grandmother's last action should have been so completely out
of character, it was only the faint rustling sound as Gil
gathered up his papers that alerted her to the fact that the
reading was over.

Dennis lounged in his chair until Gil had made his
good-byes and left for another appointment. Then he
pulled himself to his feet and, without a word to anyone,

picked up the whiskey bottle and left the study. His step was unsteady, and she heard him bumping into the wall and cursing as he lurched down the hallway to his bedroom.

Adam raked his fingers through his hair in an abrupt, angry gesture. "I see Dennis is still holding a one-man wake," he said.

Shannon stared numbly at her hands, which were tightly folded in her lap, and Ned spoke up in clarification. "He's been like that ever since his mother passed on, God rest her soul."

"Then it's high time he snapped out of it," Adam announced.

Shannon leaped to her feet to try to stop Adam as he followed after her uncle. "No, Adam," she begged. "Please leave him alone."

"Stay out of this, Shannon," Adam replied curtly. He kept on walking and she scurried after him. In her attempt to dissuade him she grabbed at his arm, but he shook off her hand and instructed her coldly, "If you want to do something useful, get your things together. I don't like being kept waiting, and I intend to take you home with me when I leave here today."

"*You* intend—" Shannon stared at Adam in disbelief. "Just like that!" she exclaimed.

"Yes, Shannon," Adam threw her own words back at her stonily. "*Just* like that."

He entered Dennis's room without bothering to knock and closed the door decisively behind him, but not before Shannon had seen the steely glint in his eyes.

She knew better than to try to defy him when he looked like that. With Alice's help she quickly packed her suitcases. Then it was a matter of waiting.

For a time she prowled from one room to another, worrying over what was happening between Adam and Dennis. Some instinct guided her to her grandmother's room. It was as austere and impersonal as the rest of the house now that it had been stripped of Agatha's belongings. Shannon started to leave, but her attention was caught by the small mountain of cartons that was neatly aligned along one wall.

Because she knew how much Alice dreaded the chore, Shannon had filled most of them herself, meticulously sealing and labeling each one. On the day after her grandmother's death, with Dennis's approval, she'd invited Alice to choose any keepsakes she would like from the glass-fronted curio cabinet that housed Agatha's collection of music boxes. Alice's eyes had filled with tears, and drying them with one corner of her apron, she'd silently shaken her head.

Later, while Shannon was sorting through the bureau drawers, Ned had come into the room and made his wife's selection for her. His gnarled forefinger stabbing toward a remarkably lifelike thrush that warbled "Bird in a Gilded Cage," he'd said, "Alice has always been partial to this one."

"I'll leave it out for her," Shannon had replied.

She had done this, and it was still on top of the bureau where she'd left it. She carefully wound the mechanism, and the song tinkled out while the thrush figurine spun in rhythm to the music, cocking its head this way and that as if it were denying responsibility for the rather tinny notes.

Shannon stood by the window staring out at the leaden sky until the music box ran down. Then she picked up the

146

carton her grandmother had wanted her to have—the one with Agatha's "memories"—and left the room.

When she reached the foyer, the front door was ajar, and she saw that Ned was just loading the last of her luggage into Adam's Mercedes. She carried the box out to be stowed with the rest of her cases.

"I can fit this in the trunk," Ned told her, "but that's about all there's space for."

Bending down to peer through the window, Shannon saw that the backseat was already piled high with garment bags. "What about my car?" she suggested.

Ned shook his head. "Adam said he'd send someone from Eagles Nest to collect the Volkswagen."

He closed the trunk, and shivering in the cold, damp air, Shannon hurried after him toward the house.

It was another hour before Adam emerged from Dennis's room. He came into the kitchen where Shannon was sitting and drinking coffee with Alice and Ned.

"Dennis could use some of that coffee," Adam said, "and some sandwiches."

Alice got to her feet. "I'll fix him a tray," she offered.

"That won't be necessary," Adam replied crisply. "He'll be coming out as soon as he's had a shower and shave."

Shannon bit her lip anxiously. "What did you say to him?" she asked.

"I told him that I expect him to be back on duty at Eagles Nest tomorrow."

"But you were with him for *hours,*" Shannon persisted. "You must have talked about something else."

Adam returned her look imperturbably. "I merely reminded him of his mother's ambition to put an end to the bad blood between the Byrnes and the MacLeods."

"And that's *all*?"

Adam nodded and one corner of his mouth quirked upward in a wry smile as he said, "You have to bear in mind that it took most of the time to sober him up so the message could get through to him."

A few minutes later Dennis himself appeared in the kitchen. He was chastened and bleary-eyed, but thanks to Adam's intervention he was obviously better prepared to pull himself together. He was pathetically grateful. He even went so far as to shake hands with Adam when they said good-bye.

By the time Shannon was seated in Adam's Mercedes for the drive to Eagles Nest, her distraction because of the new amiability between her uncle and Adam provided a temporary respite from her nervousness over taking up residence in Adam's cottage. But when Adam parked the car near the front door, her earlier tension reasserted itself, and all the while they were unloading her luggage, she was on the verge of panic.

Her fears were premature, however. After he'd carried her things inside and stacked them in the entry hall, Adam said, "I have a couple of conferences scheduled for this afternoon. I'm sorry I can't stay, but I couldn't get out of them."

"Th-that's quite all right," Shannon stammered. "I understand."

Adam hadn't sounded at all sorry, and although she felt a strange sinking sensation in her middle at the thought of his leaving her on her own, she truly did understand. The MacLeods had thoroughly monopolized his time for the past two weeks, and as a consequence he must have had to neglect his other clients.

"It's probably just as well," he remarked with madden-

148

ing cheerfulness. "It'll give you time to settle in and get your bearings."

"Y-yes," she agreed. She sensed he was looking at her, but she couldn't meet his eyes.

"If you need anything, you can call the housekeeper at the lodge."

It made her feel horribly gauche, but no matter how hard she tried, she couldn't force herself to return his gaze. She was divided against herself. Part of her wanted to strike out at Adam, while the other part wanted to draw him close and never let him leave her again.

Why is he watching me so intently? she wondered, *and what does he expect of me?* She didn't know the answers to those questions any more than she knew whether her inner turmoil was apparent to him, but she knew that if he didn't leave soon, she was going to do something foolish; something she would regret.

She felt so self-conscious that when Adam finally moved, she flinched. But he only pivoted impatiently away from her and started down the walk toward his car.

Now Shannon felt contrarily bereft because he *didn't* look at her again as he got behind the wheel. When he called, "See you later," and drove away, it was she who watched him. And though she waited for some small sign of affection—a smile, a wave of the hand—until the car was out of sight, she was disappointed.

For a long time after he'd disappeared from view, she stared after Adam, thinking that if he'd kissed her, even if he'd only given her a dutiful peck on the cheek, she might feel less awkward. She'd certainly feel less lonely.

There was an illusion of isolation about the cottage that intensified Shannon's loneliness. It was situated in a small clearing in the woods, and although the trees that crowded so closely about it were leafless at this time of year, the lodge wasn't visible from the step where she was standing.

The trees were all around her, reaching skeletal fingers toward the sky, and the wind rattled their branches like dry bones. It was hard to credit that they'd ever worn the promising green of summer or the golden mantle of autumn. They seemed sterile and incapable of making the transition to springtime.

In spite of the barrenness of the encroaching trees, it was a rain squall that drove her indoors. When the sudden downpour began, she literally ran into the living room where she huddled in a chair, clutching her raincoat about her more for protection than warmth. At first she thought it was her apprehensive mood that made the inside of the cottage appear as somber as the outside.

God! how she'd dreaded revisiting this place where she'd once been so happy and so hopeful, so full of love. This place where she'd felt so loved. It seemed a profanation to be here when she was demoralized and hopeless and unloved. She wanted to keep her memories at bay, and she tried to stop her eyes from seeing, but gradually it dawned on her that in the interval since she'd last been to the cottage, Adam had made so many changes that it was almost unrecognizable.

After she had turned on a few lights, she realized that although the room was rather dark because of its woodwork and the exposed brick of the fireplace wall, it wasn't at all gloomy. In the lamplight its color scheme of rust and cinnamon and chocolate was really quite mellow, even if it was unabashedly masculine.

Adam had replaced the red tartan carpet that was the Eagles Nest trademark with a silky Bokhara rug, and she approved of that. It was the only thing about the room that was soft, and she rewarded herself for her bravery in coming inside by kicking off her shoes and curling her stockinged toes into the thickness of the rug. She felt warmer now, and although she didn't take her raincoat off, she untied the belt and loosened the buttons.

It was curiosity that compelled her to explore the rest of the cottage. Carrying her shoes in one hand, she padded from the living room to see if Adam had made any other changes. Even before she'd turned on the lights in the hallway, the plush feel of the floor covering beneath her feet revealed that there was also new carpeting here. She stopped to admire a Chagall print before she continued along the hall.

Opening the door a crack, she peeked into the spare bedroom. It was more cluttered than she remembered, furnished with odds and ends that were obviously castoffs from the other rooms, but otherwise it was the same.

The master bedroom, on the other hand, was completely different. It was as unremittingly masculine as the living room, for various shades of brown predominated here as well, and it was walnut-paneled and neatly fitted with built-in wall units. She sat at the end of the bed, bouncing a bit to test its comfort, while her eyes surveyed the room.

In one corner, there was an earthenware jug of bittersweet berries, and this was the only bright touch in the Spartan simplicity of the room. On looking down, Shannon hastily corrected her evaluation to include the rug beside the bed.

She dropped her shoes and knelt to run her fingers over the pile of the rug. The ivory stripe that alternated with gray and beige in its bold geometric design emphasized the darkness of the rest of the room, and the weave was so thick that it was fur-like.

Her mouth curved in a bemused smile, and she asked herself, "What *is* it with Adam and rugs?"

Before she could suppress it, the memory of her wedding night sprang into her mind and she remembered Adam making love to her in the living room by the flickering glow of the fire. Her memories were so vivid that she relived the drowning sensation she'd experienced when the lean hardness of his body had pressed her body deeper and deeper into the softness of the fur-like rug that had been by the hearth. But she'd quickly forgotten about any sensations other than the sight of Adam, and the scent of him, and the taste of his kisses. Totally embraced, totally embracing, aware only of the rapture of being one with him, she'd been oblivious to everything but his closeness and his caresses and the muted sounds of their lovemaking.

But now she recalled that their marriage bed had been a furry rug, and she jumped to her feet when it occurred to her that this might be significant. She raced through the rest of the cottage, carelessly leaving lights on and slamming doors behind her. The house was not very large, and in less than a minute she was back in the bedroom, her suspicions confirmed.

Even the bathrooms and the kitchen were luxuriously carpeted. On the one time when he'd made love to her, Adam had tipped his hand, and this was one swinging bachelor's pad that was well-equipped for a pair of lovers to indulge themselves whenever and wherever the mood struck them.

For a moment Shannon was immobilized by misery. Then jealousy boiled up inside her, driving out everything but the awful need to find some kind of tangible proof of Adam's faithlessness.

She knew she was snooping, and she no longer made any attempt to justify it. She began with the bathroom that adjoined his bedroom, quickly returning to the bedroom when she found nothing out of the ordinary in the medicine cabinet or linen closet. With each drawer or closet door she opened, her fury waned a bit, but just when relief was beginning to outweigh anger, on a shelf high up in the wardrobe she found what she was looking for.

She had to stand on a chair to retrieve the evidence, and her hands were shaking so badly that she dropped it. She felt giddy, and after she climbed off the chair she rested for a few seconds, closing her eyes and leaning her forehead against the cool paneling of the door.

She hadn't really believed that a man with Adam's strong appetites would have lived like a monk for more than seven years. They'd never discussed the past, but she knew there had been other women before her. Gil Rutherford had told her as much. "The women Adam seemed to prefer were the ones who knew the score," he'd said. "That's why I was so surprised when Adam began going out with you."

On the day she'd met with Adam at his office he'd been quick to accuse her of infidelity and when he had said he no longer needed "romance" to be happy, she'd been skeptical. She'd told herself the word "romance" was a euphemism for one-night stands. She had suspected that Adam hadn't been celibate for seven *days,* let alone seven years, and she had thought she could cope with that. But it was one thing to suspect; it was quite another to *know* that she was only one of a long line of women who had warmed his bed.

"And I probably won't be the *last,*" she muttered irately

as she began poking around in the back of the closet for the article she had dropped.

What she'd found was a lady's high-heeled evening sandal, and she supposed that under normal circumstances she wouldn't have considered it at all sinister. But the circumstances were far from normal. And now, as if she hadn't enough problems, she couldn't find the damned thing! As if the fates had conspired against her, her eyes were filled with self-pitying tears, and because the sandal was black, it was camouflaged by the dark-stained planking of the closet floor.

"Looking for something?"

The question was issued in Adam's deep-toned drawl just when, at long last, Shannon located the sandal. She started guiltily and glanced at him over her shoulder. Her cheeks were flushed, and her eyes were feverishly bright as they skidded over the strong length of his thighs, encased in narrow-fitting gray trousers.

His stance was threatening, with his feet solidly planted and his hands on his hips, fingers splayed. His trench coat was open and her eyes moved timidly upward over his white shirt front toward his face.

The shoulders of the coat were damp, and raindrops glistened in his hair. His eyes were dark and implacable, and he looked very tall and imposing as he stood over her. She got to her feet and tried to sidestep him, but he shifted with her, imprisoning her in the closet doorway.

"As a matter of fact I was looking for this," she replied breathlessly, holding out the sandal.

Her heart pounding in her throat, she watched the dawning recognition in his face as he studied the sandal. Unexpectedly he chuckled, and goaded by his laughter, Shannon exclaimed hotly, "It's quite a charming style, but it's a little outdated. Besides, I don't think it would go with the rest of your wardrobe. I mean, let's face it, it's just not you!"

"I'm relieved to hear that," Adam countered sardonically, "but I can't understand why you'd think it was mine." He took the shoe from her and examined it more closely. The dainty patent-leather evening slipper was dwarfed by his hand, and he smiled whimsically as he declared, "It's obviously not my size."

"Then what was it doing in your closet?"

"A certain young lady lost it on my front step one midnight. She was on her way home from the ball, but she was stranded when her coach turned into a pumpkin."

Grinning mischievously at Shannon's puzzled frown, his eyes shining with amusement, Adam bowed from the waist and offered her his elbow. She automatically took his arm and found herself being escorted to the bed. When she was seated, he dropped to his knees in front of her. "Allow me, Cinderella," he said, and adroitly slipped the sandal onto her foot.

"It's mine!" she whispered. "I thought—"

Her breath caught in her throat when the backs of Adam's fingers brushed her skin while he was fastening the buckle. His fingers closed about her ankle, effectively guaranteeing her continued silence. A searing shock of desire shot along her nerve endings at the scalding touch of his hand. In an effort to deny her longing for him, she kept her face averted and tried to smooth her skirt primly over her knees, but his hand stilled hers.

"I know what you thought," he said softly, "but I'd be interested in hearing *why* you thought it."

His voice was so gentle that tears rushed to her eyes,

and before she could compose herself they were rolling down her cheeks.

"Oh, damn!" she mumbled. She wanted to hide her face before the trickle of tears became a deluge, and she tried to pull her hand away from Adam, but his grip on it tightened.

"Why, Shannon?" he insisted.

She shook her head helplessly. "The rugs," she began, "they're so—so—"

"I think I get the picture," he said dryly. "I have to admit that I went overboard when I decorated the bedroom."

She risked a glance at him and blushed when she saw the contemplative way he was studying her.

"Do you want to know if you're going to have to contend with any of my old flames? Have you been wondering if I've been abstinent?"

Her face crumpled and she looked away from him, embarrassed by the endless stream of tears. It seemed vitally important that he should not guess that she was jealous.

"It doesn't matter," she said dully.

"No," he agreed evenly, "it doesn't. But I have a theory about these rugs. Perhaps you'd find it entertaining."

"I don't really give a damn why—"

"I notice you've reverted to form," he cut in smoothly. "I'll bet you had your shoes off before you'd been in the house for ten minutes. I banked on that. I hoped you'd find it impossible to resist the temptation. You see, Shannon, I attribute your sensational legs to your addiction to going barefoot, and the rugs are intended to encourage you never to break the habit."

One of his hands released hers to trail seductively along

156

her thigh to her knee. When he reached the hem of her skirt, he reversed directions, sliding his hand lazily under the fabric and kindling a line of fire as he moved it back toward her hips.

Mesmerized by his touch, she sat perfectly still. She was vaguely aware that with his other hand he was removing the pins from her hair. When this was done, his fingers curved around the nape of her neck and he bent his head, replacing the touch of his fingers with his mouth, nuzzling the sensitive hollows of her throat and teasing them moistly with the tip of his tongue.

His lips were sending sweet darts of pleasure through her as they moved along the side of her neck. His hand was intimately molding her thigh, and with the least touch of his knowing fingers, with the tantalizing warmth of his mouth, he was awakening long-dormant responses that she was powerless to suppress. Her hands were flattened against his chest as if she would push him away, but she could feel his heart racing in concert with hers, and with every throbbing beat her resistance to him was growing weaker.

His lips traveled across her cheek toward her mouth, and even the slight raspiness of the stubble on his chin was delicious. His lips claimed hers, gently at first, feathering lightly and insistently from side to side as they savored the passionate trembling of hers. Then their breaths mingled in a sigh and his open mouth crushed hers almost violently, while his tongue probed deeply, avidly feeding on the sweetness of her lips.

He eased her backward onto the bed, parting her thighs with his knee and pinning them with the weight of his thighs, urgently fitting his hips to hers so that she could feel his arousal. Somehow his hand had found its way inside her coat and under her sweater and was exploring the silken softness of her skin. She tensed with anticipation as his hand began inching slowly upward over her rib cage. She heard the ragged intake of his breath when he reached the delicate undercurve of her breast and discovered that she was not wearing a bra. He hesitated briefly, surprised to find that she was naked beneath the sweater, then his hand cupped her breast fully. He was a little rough in his eagerness, almost desperate, as if he were starving for the touch of her.

Suddenly they were locked together in a tangle of limbs and clothing, and their writhing bodies were straining to be even closer. But their frantic attempts were frustrated by the layers of material that separated them.

When the doorbell rang, they lay still for a moment, panting for breath, their foreheads touching as they stared into each other's eyes, each of them trying to disavow the unwanted intrusion.

The doorbell rang again, and Adam savagely muttered an oath. For another instant his hand lingered at her breast, then, sighing resignedly, he disengaged his arms from around her, planted a kiss at the corner of her mouth, and rolled off the bed.

When the bell sounded a third time, he smiled wryly, a bit arrogantly, at her as he combed his hair with his fingers.

"This is a hell of a note," he growled, "but don't go away. Whoever it is, I'll get rid of them."

She watched him while he straightened his clothing, and the sight of him filled her with a pleasure that was so intense it caused an ache deep within her.

As he left the room Adam quipped, "It's a good thing I'm still wearing my coat!"

CHAPTER ELEVEN

The effect of Adam's laughing comment was chilling. As soon as the door closed behind him, Shannon sat up and swung her feet to the floor. She pulled off the sandal without bothering to undo the buckle, tearing the strap loose in the process. As if she needed to destroy the evidence of her folly, she quickly smoothed the spread over the bed and slipped on her shoes. Before she stumbled into the bathroom, she hunted for her hairpins, but she could find only two of them.

Her mind was functioning with painful clarity, and she decided it would be a meaningless, childish gesture to lock the door, so she left it open.

She stood at the basin, staring at her reflection as she turned on the cold tap and let the water run over her wrists to cool her inflamed senses. What she saw in the mirror sickened her, for her eyes were slumbrous with passion, her lips were swollen from Adam's kisses, and her hair was hanging half over her face. She tossed it back angrily.

She was appalled that she'd behaved so wantonly. They'd been rolling around on the bed, groping one another like a couple of sex-starved adolescents, and all the while they'd been *fully dressed,* right down to their *coats.*

159

It was this that made the whole episode seem shameful and sordid.

Pushing her hands through her hair, she gathered fistfuls of it and skinned it back cruelly, punishing her scalp as she would like to punish her woman's body for its treachery.

"God, but you're ludicrous!" she contemptuously told her image.

She was no longer a silly teen-ager with stars in her eyes, ready to fall into her idol's arms at the drop of a hat—or a shoe. She no longer believed in fairy-tale endings, yet she'd been so taken in by Adam's charm, so *turned on* by his raw masculinity, that she'd allowed him to tumble her on the bed as if he were playing the prince to her Cinderella.

She had always been easy for him, so easy that he had assumed she was that way with other men, but she had been idiotic enough to believe that this time it would be different. She had promised herself that she would be cautious. She'd admitted the likelihood that Adam might never regard her as anything more than a temporary mistress, but she had vowed that she would remain the mistress of her own emotions. Foolishly she had concluded that if she couldn't have Adam's love, she would at least earn his respect.

A few minutes later Adam came into the bedroom to find Shannon at the bureau, composedly combing the snarls out of her hair. She watched him through the mirror and saw the almost boyish look of eagerness leave his expression when he discovered that she was not waiting for him in the bed, but if he was brokenhearted over her change of mind, he hid it well.

He had stopped to remove his coat—as she had—and

when he realized that the fun and games were over, he shrugged out of his suit jacket, pulled off his necktie, and hung them away in the closet. This accomplished, he undid his collar button and began folding back his shirt sleeves.

"Who was at the door?" Shannon asked, proud of her casual tone.

"Sam Watson," Adam replied. "He just drove your VW over from Shagbark and he wanted to deliver the keys."

Now that she'd made the mistake of attracting his attention, Adam held her eyes in the mirror as he sauntered toward the bureau. His gaze was steady and he smiled thinly. "Changed your mind, have you?"

Shannon licked her dry lips and replaced the comb next to Adam's military brushes. "The cottage is so tidy," she observed brightly. "I can see I'll have to be on my toes to come up to such high standards."

"That won't be necessary," Adam said tersely. "The housekeeper at the lodge handles all the cleaning."

To cover her consternation, Shannon realigned the comb so that it was angled as precisely as the brushes. A worried frown ruffled the smoothness of her forehead.

"I'll have to find something to do to fill my days," she remarked. "Walt Hensley suggested that I apply at the grade school to be called in as a substitute. He said they were shorthanded."

"That sounds like a good idea." Adam glanced down at her left hand and reached out to lightly touch the third finger. "We'll have to see about getting a new wedding ring for you."

Shannon shook her head, sending her silky hair flying about her slender shoulders. "I still have my old ring. I prefer to wear it." She looked shyly at Adam. "I have

161

something of yours, too. It's with the rest of my luggage in the entry hall.''

"I noticed you haven't gotten around to unpacking," Adam said coolly. "Does that mean you're not certain whether you'll stay?"

Shannon stared at him, not knowing how to answer. "I'll get my ring," she announced, and hastily left the bedroom.

When she returned, Adam was stretched out on the bed, sleeping soundly. He hadn't even bothered to turn back the spread. She slipped the wedding ring on her finger and left the box with the terry cloth robe on the nightstand. She envied the ease with which Adam had put what had happened between them out of his mind; in fact, she resented it. But she found a blanket to put over him before she tiptoed out of the room.

He slept for more than two hours, not waking until eight o'clock. Shannon was curled up on the living room sofa, watching a movie on television, and when the station break came on, she looked up to see Adam in the doorway. He was yawning and stretching hugely, but he looked more rested, if slightly rumpled. His hair was tousled and, she decided critically, he needed a shave.

He eyed the glass of wine on the end table beside her. "A little Dutch courage?" he inquired.

"I am a little nervous," she conceded stiffly, annoyed that he'd read her mood so accurately. "May I get you something to drink?"

"No, thanks. I'll help myself if I want anything."

He hadn't mentioned the robe, and she wondered if this meant he hadn't seen it or that he just didn't give a damn. She was irritated because she was afraid his omission was for the latter reason, and her tone was withering as she asked, "Did you know there's nothing in your refrigerator but a dried-out wedge of cheese and a can of tomato juice?"

"No, I didn't," Adam answered blandly, refusing to be withered. "For the past week or two I've been too busy to make an inventory."

At this reference to the amount of time he'd spent with her, Shannon was conscience-stricken. "I was going to fix dinner," she explained.

"There's probably a steak in the freezer."

She felt like weeping from sheer frustration. "It would take *hours* to thaw a steak!"

Adam shrugged. "We can always have dinner at the lodge," he said.

"No," she snapped. "I'd rather not."

"Then we can warm up some TV dinners. There must be a couple of them left."

It was apparent that Adam considered the debate closed, for he picked up the evening newspaper and, leaning back in his chair, unfurled the editorial section between them.

Since he had denied her the opportunity to expend her temper in a verbal battle with him, Shannon went into the kitchen and took out her anger on the cupboards as she looked through them for something that would make an adequate meal. She felt vindicated when she found that Adam was mistaken and that there were no TV dinners in the freezer compartment; there were only the steak and some cans of concentrated orange juice.

Muttering, slamming doors, and banging pots and pans, Shannon rummaged through the cabinets. She found a package of crackers, a can of cocktail peanuts, more tomato juice, olives, instant coffee and creamer, several jars of caviar, and several more of pâté. The noise she made reached a new crescendo with each cupboard she searched, and when she had finished, she stalked back into the living room and waited, her spine ramrod straight, until Adam lowered the paper to glance at her quizzically.

"What's wrong now?" he asked.

"Don't you *ever* eat anything but cocktail-party food?" Shannon exclaimed. "Don't you have regular meals."

"I've been eating out most of the time."

"Well, it's a wonder you're not suffering from malnutrition," she grumbled. "I've never seen such empty cupboards!"

"I'm sure you'll do your best to change all that," Adam replied brusquely.

"Is that what you want me to do?"

"Not particularly."

He replaced the barrier of the paper with a snap of finality, and the fight drained out of Shannon. She acknowledged that she had been cleverly outmaneuvered by Adam's refusal to join the fray. She sank down onto the sofa with a defeated air, and for a few minutes she was silent, pleating her skirt with her fingers and stealing an occasional look at her husband. Finally she decided she could no longer bear the ambiguity of her position, and she asked softly, "What *do* you expect of me, Adam?"

Again the paper was lowered, and this time he folded it and looked at her challengingly. "What do you think I expect?"

"I don't know," Shannon slowly replied. "You've pointed out that you don't need a wife to care for your home or cook your meals."

Adam smiled. "Perhaps all I want is your body."

"No," she said pensively. "I don't think that's it either.

If sex was your only reason, there must be any number of women who'd jump at the chance to share your bed without your having to put up with all the hassles of marriage."

"Thanks for that vote of confidence," Adam gibed, "but you do realize you're running out of motives, don't you." He'd stopped smiling and his mouth was set and hard. "Do you think Agatha insisted that we make another try at marriage as a condition of naming me in her will?"

Shannon shook her head. "I don't think that either Shagbark or Eagles Nest are so important to you that you'd sacrifice your freedom for them."

Adam was placated, and he laughed softly. "We're narrowing it down, at least. So far, we've ruled out free labor, sex, and material gain. Suppose you tell me what's left."

"There's the feud," Shannon conjectured gravely. "You might give up your freedom to end that."

For a full minute Adam was so quiet that she thought he hadn't heard her. Then, although he hadn't moved a muscle and his expression hadn't changed, she sensed that his anger was like a tightly coiled spring that had been wound beyond endurance and was about to break.

"Damn the feud!" he exclaimed fiercely. In one lithe movement he tossed the newspaper aside and was on his feet, striding toward the front hall.

Wondering at her temerity in provoking him, Shannon followed in his wake. "Wh-where are you going?" she stammered.

"To the lodge for dinner," he replied shortly. "If you decide you want to join me, feel free."

She made no further move to detain him as he grabbed his raincoat from the coat rack, hooked it over his shoulder, and left the cottage. But after he'd gone, she stood in

165

the open door, trembling and peering after him until he had disappeared into the darkness. When he was safely out of hearing range, in a timid token of defiance she called stridently and so loudly that it hurt her throat, "Don't hold your breath, Adam Byrne, because I won't join you!"

She closed the door and leaned against it to steady herself.

"*I won't!*" she repeated brokenly, in a whisper that echoed and reechoed through the empty rooms, until it seemed to her that the cottage was mocking her loneliness.

Shannon cried herself to sleep that night. The thought of Adam's reaction when he came home and discovered she still hadn't unpacked was cause for concern, but she hadn't the heart to make a beginning. She moved her overnight case into the spare room, thankful that Alice had had the foresight to suggest that she keep her night things separate from the rest of her clothing.

The tears started when she opened the case and saw the nightgown Alice had packed for her. Fashioned of diaphanous white chiffon with lace insets, it was the prettiest, most bridelike one she owned, and she wondered why she hadn't had the good sense to guess that Alice might pull such a stunt.

Seven years ago she'd had her wedding night and no nightdress, and she laughed through her tears at her own stupidity, at the ironic twist of fate that had provided her with a gown suitable for a wedding night when there would be none.

It seemed that nothing was destined to go smoothly for her that night. The bed was made up only with a throw, and she couldn't find any sheets in the cottage, but there was a pillow and there was the extra blanket in the master bedroom. That would have to do, she decided, because there was no way that she was going to sleep with Adam.

As she stood under the stinging spray of the shower, she felt so completely drained by the emotional turbulence of the day that she thought she'd never be able to cry again. It wasn't until she'd slipped into the nightgown and was lying on the narrow bed in the darkened bedroom that the nagging sense of isolation returned to plague her.

The silence of the cottage was so palpable that it drummed against her ears and pounded inside her head. Loneliness engulfed and oppressed her until she felt that she was being suffocated by it. She felt as if she were being entombed, and she counted her heartbeats to confirm that she was still alive. Then she realized that she was crying again, and the tears reassured her, for they were another means of validating that she wasn't dead. Wrapping herself in the blanket, she gave herself over to the storm of weeping until she fell into an exhausted, dreamless sleep.

When Adam burst into the room an hour or so later, Shannon thought at first that it was morning. Then she recognized that it was the undiffused glare of the overhead light and not the sun that was shining onto her closed eyelids.

She murmured protestingly and tried to pull the blanket over her head, only to have it torn rudely away from her. Deprived of the blanket, clad only in her thin nightdress, she shivered and tried to curl her body into the warmth of the spread at her back, but she was thwarted when a hand was inserted, none too gently, beneath her shoulders, while another one was under her knees and she was being lifted into the air.

The hardness of a shoulder replaced her pillow, and a pair of powerful arms cradled her against the delicious warmth of a broad chest. Instinctively clinging to the muscular shoulders, she snuggled closer. Even when she half-opened her eyes, her mind was still fogged with sleep. She looked drowsily up at Adam, and her thoughts were in such disorder that she wasn't immediately conscious of anything but contentment that he was holding her and a profound sense of belonging.

It wasn't until the Chagall print drifted through her line of vision that she became aware that Adam had carried her into the hall. She stiffened in his arms. Her hands no longer clung to him. She was fully alert, but her voice was husky with sleep as she cried, "Put me down!"

"Not a chance!" Adam's arms tightened pitilessly about her.

"Wh-what are you doing?"

"I'm taking you where you belong," he declared. "To my bed."

"B-but nothing is settled. We have to talk."

"No!" he exclaimed, his voice booming. "We've done nothing but talk all night. Now we're going to do things *my* way and try some action!"

He turned into his room, his pace so brisk that she was dizzied by it, and kicked the door shut behind him. He dumped her unceremoniously onto the bed, and she lay where she'd landed, scowling up at him while she tried to recover her equilibrium.

His face was as dark as a thundercloud, and his ferocious expression made him seem a frightening stranger. The alarm that jolted through her prompted Shannon to try to escape, and she rolled away from Adam and somersaulted off the far side of the bed. Landing on her feet, she whirled around to confront him.

For a few seconds they stared at one another warily.

Shannon was gasping for breath, her breasts heaving as if she'd been running for miles, and her breathing became even more labored when Adam smiled mockingly. He began circling the bed toward her, blocking the path to the door, and she realized that he was amused by her ineffectual attempt to elude him.

"I told you once that you're my woman," he proclaimed caustically, "and I'm damned tired of waiting for you to grow up!"

"*You're* tired!" she retorted shrilly. "If you were so blasted anxious to exercise your husbandly rights, why wouldn't you see me after the fire?"

"*I tried to, damn it!*"

Adam's tone was so stentorian that it made Shannon's ears ring, but it was the meaning of his reply that stunned her into momentary speechlessness. She even stopped backing away from him.

Timorously she argued, "Alice said—"

"Alice lied to you," Adam brusquely interrupted. "When I came by Shagbark the morning after the fire, I asked to speak to you and Agatha told me that you didn't want to see me."

Shannon wanted more than anything to believe him, but she was staggered by the idea that her grandmother could have betrayed her, and she shook her head. Then she looked at Adam's face and she knew that he'd spoken the truth.

She felt very cold, as if she were in shock. Her hands and feet were icy and she was shivering. And even though Adam was still stalking her, she was incapable of moving. The chill temperature of the bedroom was lapping about her, and she was reminded of the thinness of her nightgown when Adam's eyes began roaming over her.

When his eyes reached her breasts, they lingered and seemed to burn her through the lacy bodice. Under his ardent gaze her own eyes wandered downward, and for the first time she noticed that he was wearing only pajama bottoms. Except for the ankh, he was naked from the waist up, but he didn't seem affected by the cold. Without his shirt his chest looked massive.

"Try not to be too hard on your grandmother, Shannon," Adam advised her, not unsympathetically. "She thought what she did was for your own good. As for Alice—" He shrugged. "She was caught in the middle."

Shannon couldn't seem to tear her eyes away from the medallion. "B-but later," she whispered. "I called you, Adam. I wrote to you."

"I was young and I was proud," he returned flatly, explaining but not excusing himself, and definitely not pleading. "I wanted your undivided loyalty, and I thought if I couldn't have that, I wanted nothing to do with you."

"And you don't feel that way now?"

He shook his head. "I've learned that only a fool expects perfection."

"What if I told you that I hadn't been disloyal to you? Would you believe that I never intended to harm you when I took your medallion?"

"Then why did you take it?"

"Because *I* was young, and I thought—" Shannon hesitated, agonizing over whether she should tell him the complete truth.

"You needn't explain," Adam suddenly relented. "I believe you, and I guess I should have known your uncle was lying. Lord knows it's consistent!" He smiled crookedly. "Can you understand why I didn't see through his lies?"

"I understand," she answered woodenly. "But it really doesn't change a thing."

"Damn it, Shannon!" he roared. Because she was still looking at the ankh, he caught her unprepared as he closed the space between them. His hands were gripping her upper arms, he was glowering down at her, and his face was flushed with anger, but his eyes were hot with desire and she could feel the heat radiating from his body. Through gritted teeth he muttered, "You are, without a doubt, the most infuriating woman I've ever known. God knows why I want you, but I do. And you want me!"

"No!" She started to shake her head, but Adam clamped her face between the hard vise of his palms and tipped her head back, forcing her to look at him.

"You love me," he insisted. "Admit it."

"No, no, no!" she chanted, her voice rising to the point of hysteria.

Still holding her so that she couldn't evade him, Adam brought his face close to hers and demanded, "Then why haven't you found someone else? Why were you jealous when you found the shoe in my closet? Why did you keep my robe? Earlier, when I was asleep, why did you take the trouble to put the blanket over me?"

"All right," she wailed. "*All right!* Even if it is only some sort of ego trip for you at my expense, I'll say it. I love you!" Adam's hold on her slackened a bit, and she twisted away from him. Turning her back on him, she added, "But what difference does that make?"

"It makes a hell of a difference to me!" he shouted. "Dammit all, Shannon, I love you, too!"

Her head snapped up. Had she heard him correctly, or had she only imagined that he'd said he loved her?

"Wh-what did you say?"

171

"I said, *I love you,* damn it!" He was still exasperated but his voice was more controlled, not as incensed. "*Now* will you come to bed?"

Slowly, still not quite believing that she hadn't misunderstood, Shannon turned to face him. He held his arms out to her, but still she hesitated. "Adam—" she began tentatively, her voice faint with surprise.

"Come here, Shannon."

The invitation was gently given, and with a single step the gap between them was bridged and Adam was holding her in his arms again, lifting her and carrying her to the bed.

He put her down tenderly and sat on the edge of the bed beside her. Still afraid that this might be an illusion, she looked up at him, and he began touching her face and running his hands lightly, wonderingly, over the curving outlines of her body.

To reassure herself that she wasn't dreaming, she reached out to touch him. The warmth and suppleness of his skin beneath her fingertips, the roughness of the hair on his chest, told her that he was very solid and real and not some romantic specter, and the slight tremor in his hands as he eased the straps of her nightgown off her shoulders and slipped it away from her told her of his desire.

For a moment he caressed her only with his eyes, but she was warmed by the love and excitement in them.

"Oh, babe, I love you so much and it's been so damned long." Adam wrapped his arms around her and lay on the bed with her, pinning her body with his, touching her all over, touching her intimately. "Have you any idea how many times I've come close to raping you?" he groaned. "The day you got home, at the supper club, that day at

172

my office—" He trailed into silence, inhaling raggedly, and Shannon cried, "Yes, Adam, yes!"

They could wait no longer. His mouth claimed hers roughly, with fast-rising urgency, and she abandoned herself to the hard thrust of his body against hers, drawing him close and closer still, as if she would absorb him through her pores.

In the same moment that Adam deepened his possession of her lips, he took her body. Compelled by mutual need, intoxicated by each other, ravenous for each other, they were swept up in a maelstrom of desire that brought them together swiftly and left them devastated with the violence of completion, and when it was over, they were far from satisfied, for release had come too soon and each of them wanted more.

Their limbs were languid and heavy, and they remained entwined with each other, too shaken to move, embracing without speaking, fanning the glowing embers of desire with soft kisses and touches, exploring and fondling each other until the flames of passion burned brightly once again.

Adam's mouth and his hands became more demanding, but now he tended the fires of passion carefully, almost worshipfully, as if he would brand Shannon with his possession and mark her eternally as his. Long after he knew that she was ready for him, he held back. With hard-won restraint he teased her, tantalizing her with the sweet volatility of his mouth, tonguing her nipples and stroking her thighs until the need for him coursed through her veins so hotly that she was consumed by it. And when her craving for him had become a torment and he moved over her, he prolonged her anticipation, bringing her to the brink of ecstasy again and again, drawing her back at the last moment, until his lovemaking had ignited a wildfire that purified their love.

Slights were forgiven, old wounds were healed, the pain of their long separation was forgotten, and they were part of the fire, as it was part of them—as they were part of each other.

Even after passion had blazed out of control, leaving them blissfully spent, they were part of each other. They were no longer two separate people, but one ecstatic being, made complete by their joining.

At last, reluctantly, they moved apart, but only for as long as it took them to turn out the lights and climb under the covers. They snuggled together sleepily. Shannon nestled close to Adam with her head on his shoulder, encompassed by the warm circle of his arms.

"Did I hurt you?" he whispered anxiously when he felt the dampness of her tears. "I'm sorry, babe. I would have been more considerate, but you made me forget how inexperienced you are."

"Don't be sorry," she replied shakily. "It's just that I'm so happy." Adam relaxed, and she turned her head to brush her lips against his skin. "Besides," she admitted shyly, "I enjoyed it."

Enchanted by her shyness, delighted by her candor, Adam hugged her even closer. "Yes, my sexy little wife," he laughed softly. "I could tell you did."

CHAPTER TWELVE

It was the following morning, when Shannon was entering the date of Agatha's death in the family Bible, that she discovered the old contract of sale. It had been stuffed loosely between the pages, and when she closed the Bible, preparing to put it away, the contract fluttered to the living room floor.

The agreement dated from the mid-1840s. It was written in a crabbed, spidery hand on heavy vellum-like paper, and Shannon had to read it through several times before she realized that what she'd found explained her grandmother's odd division of the Shagbark acreage.

The document spelled out the conditions for the purchase of the MacLeod lands along the river bluffs—lands that were now among the finest ski slopes in the region. A legal description of the property for which title was to be transferred was included. The grantor was Liam MacLeod and the grantee was Noah Byrne. Admittedly it was informal, but it appeared to Shannon that the agreement was legally binding. The signatures had even been witnessed, although the names of the witnesses were unfamiliar to her.

As soon as she recognized the significance of her find, she rushed into the bedroom.

"Adam, wake up and look at this!" she caroled gaily.

Adam opened one eye and looked at her for a moment. Without warning his arm hooked around her waist and he toppled her onto the bed. His nearness made her forget about the contract, and it slipped from her fingers as she settled her slight weight more comfortably on top of him.

Raising an eyebrow at her, he grinned and inquired, "What are you doing up so early?"

"It's not early. It's almost nine thirty, and I have a lot to do today."

"The first of which is to satisfy your greedy husband." He nibbled delicately at her earlobe. "Ummm, you smell good. What's that perfume you're wearing?"

She sniffed at her forearm and laughed. "That's not perfume. That's only soap from my shower."

The tip of his tongue flicked along the side of her neck. "It isn't soap," he countered. "It tastes too good."

Shannon wrinkled her nose at him. "Then maybe it's me," she suggested throatily.

"Whatever it is, it's delightful." His hands wandered over her back to her hips. "So you're not wearing perfume," he mused as he molded her closer to him, "and unless my hands deceive me, you're not wearing anything else under that robe."

"Please, Adam—"

"I know." He smiled indolently. "You still have to unpack. But it's already waited this long, so it can wait a while longer."

"I suppose the unpacking can wait," she agreed, "but there's still no food in the house and I'm hungry."

"Hungry!" he exclaimed dryly. "And here I thought you were a romantic. I'd planned for us to live on love."

"Sounds heavenly!" Shannon sighed weakly and Adam

tried to kiss her, but she placed her fingertips against his mouth to fend him off and said with mock sternness, "Now, try telling that to my stomach!"

In the next instant Adam had turned her onto her back and was whispering something in the region of her midriff.

"What *are* you doing?" Shannon asked.

"Telling it to your stomach," he replied solemnly. He pressed his ear to her middle, and she laughed helplessly at his intent expression.

"Shhh!" he ordered. "I can't hear what it's saying."

For a few more seconds he pretended to be listening, then he nodded thoughtfully and lay down beside her. As he gathered her close she prompted breathlessly, "Well? What does it say?"

"It says another hour, more or less, won't make that much difference."

Adam was already untying the belt of her robe, and the touch of his hands made her heart sing. Her plans for the day no longer seemed at all important.

"You must be brilliant in the courtroom," she complimented him huskily. "You're very persuasive."

"I can be persuasive in the bedroom, too."

"I know! I know!" Shannon retorted saucily, and they laughed together at his lack of modesty.

His eyes were suddenly alight with a mixture of deviltry and passion, for he'd learned that he was right in his assumption that she was naked except for the robe. Her smile faded and her breath constricted with excitement as his hands stroked over her breasts, coaxing the nipples to tautness. She arched into his touch and pressed closer to him.

"Adam," she murmured.

"Hmmm?"

"Persuade *me*," she invited in a small voice.

Adam stopped nuzzling her ear and smiled down at her. "Sweetheart," he replied gruffly, one corner of his mouth twitching in a passable Bogart imitation, "I think I already have."

They were leaving the coffee shop at the lodge before Shannon remembered the contract. By the time they'd left the cottage, it was almost noon, so they'd had brunch instead of breakfast, and she was so utterly contented, so replete with love and food, she felt like purring.

They saw Dennis across the lobby and waved to him. He responded cheerfully and appeared to be fully recovered from his bout of melancholic inertia. The sight of her uncle jogged Shannon's memory, and she told Adam about the document she'd found in the Bible, describing it in detail. In her enthusiasm the words spilled out in a torrent, and she was astonished when Adam said calmly, "I'm familiar with the contract."

"You know about the sale?" she exclaimed. "But how?"

"Come for a walk with me, and I'll tell you."

He helped her into her coat, buttoning it snugly under her chin and turning the collar up for extra warmth, and they left the lodge, following the walkway that led to the back terrace.

The world had never looked so beautiful. The sky was a clear and brilliant blue, fresh-washed by the rain, and gusty breezes out of the north had caused the temperature to plunge into the teens. Even the branches of the trees, the shrubs that lined the path, the blades of grass in the lawn, were transformed into things of beauty, for they were encrusted with a thin layer of ice that sparkled like diamonds in the sunlight.

When they reached the trail to the river, Adam hesitated and glanced down at Shannon. "Are you sure you're warm enough?" he inquired.

She nodded. He had tucked one of her hands into the pocket of his parka, where he continued to hold it, and she was warmed by his concern for her well-being.

They started down the trail, Adam shortening his stride to accommodate to hers. "Dad said he'd shown you the eyrie and told you a little about it," he remarked.

"Yes, he did," Shannon replied. She wondered what the nest had to do with the agreement she'd found, but Adam said nothing more as they walked down the steep slope toward the edge of the bluff.

He knew the ground they were covering well enough to hike it blindfolded, and he kept his eyes fixed on the dead elm, on the ice-spangled eyrie that was cradled in a fork at the top of the tree. The nest was swaying hypnotically in the breeze, and relying on Adam to guide her safely, Shannon began watching it also. When they arrived at the elm, Adam continued to stare up at the eyrie.

"This is one elm that wasn't killed by Dutch elm disease." With his free hand he gave the trunk of the tree an affectionate pat. "It was the weight of the nest that killed it. It must weigh a ton."

Shannon admired Adam while he admired the tree. Although he still held her hand, in his concentration on the elm he seemed to have forgotten about her, and she felt a twinge of jealousy. Was this her real rival, she wondered, and if it was, how could she compete with it? *My God,* she thought irrelevantly, *I have met the enemy, and he's a tree!*

She studied the elm curiously. It was a giant, she acknowledged. It was much taller than any of its companions, and even at eye level it was a good three feet in diameter. She could easily imagine how impressive it must have been when it was alive, standing like a sentinel at the edge of the bluff. Perhaps, had it found a more hospitable environment, a place where it hadn't had to contend so tenaciously with the elements, it would even have reached record proportions.

But it was only a snag, after all, and it was full of rot. Once it had harbored eagles, but now it was teeming with insect parasites. It was riddled with their burrows. Soon— maybe this very winter—the weight of the snow or the wind would overburden the tree and it would fall.

It seemed Adam was keenly aware of this possibility, for he had peeled away a loose scab of bark and was crumbling it between his fingers.

"I doubt if there's any creature with more symbolism about it than the eagle," he said nostalgically. "When I was a kid, I was intrigued by them for all the obvious reasons. They're powerful and noble and wild, and yet they present a paradox because once they've taken a mate, their faithfulness to one another and to their young is awesome. And the nest seems to call them back to it almost magnetically."

He opened his hand to cast the crumbled bark upon the wind, and sensing his sadness, Shannon turned to look at him.

"In a very real sense," he continued abstractedly, "eagles aren't free at all. They're bound by chains of instinct to the territory, to the eyrie, and to their mate. But they give the impression that there's a great deal of devotion within the family group, so in many ways their servitude seems wholly voluntary."

Adam was standing with his head thrown back so that he could see the eyrie so far above them, and Shannon was struck by the sharp contrast between the way of life of the eagles and his own upbringing. As a boy, with his mother rarely around and his father ignoring him, Adam's observation of the eyrie must have given him insight into family life of a very different sort from his.

How sad, Shannon thought, that it should have taken wild creatures to show him this. She mourned for the boy Adam had been, and she vowed that some day, somehow, she would make up for all that he'd missed.

While she was making this vow, Adam glanced at her. He saw the tears that had gathered on her lashes and pulled her close.

"Are you crying for me?" he asked incredulously.

Nodding, Shannon slipped her arms inside his parka and wrapped them around his waist while he dried her tears with kisses. He felt her trembling and shifted so that she was protected from the wind by his body.

"You're cold!" he exclaimed. "Let's get out of the wind and I'll explain the connection between the agreement you found and the eagles."

Hand in hand they moved uphill to a sheltered glade that was ringed by pines. The sun had dried the grass, and they seated themselves with their backs against a moss-covered boulder. After a moment Adam stretched out on the ground with his arms folded over his chest, hands laced, and his head pillowed in Shannon's lap. He was still looking up at the eyrie, and for a while he was silent.

Shannon had never seen Adam so completely relaxed, and feeling strangely protective, she stroked his hair away from his forehead, enjoying its springy texture and the way it curled so crisply around her fingers. She liked to look at him when he was unaware that he was being observed. She loved the boldness of his craggy, uneven features.

After a bit, however, she pulled at his hair gently, prompting him to give her the promised explanation.

"Adam, *please!*" she exclaimed, "Tell me—"

"Okay," he said, laughing at her impatience. "It's really very simple. Noah Byrne was in his eighties when he bought that land from Liam MacLeod, but he still had all his wits about him, so the copy you found—Liam's copy—wasn't the only one. Noah had one as well, and he was on his way into Galena to record the deed when his carriage overturned and he was killed."

"Why didn't one of his family take care of the paperwork?" asked Shannon.

"Because they had no proof the deal had been finalized. From what I've been able to discover, it was raining that day, and Noah had rolled up the contract and wrapped it in oilcloth to protect it from the weather. It must have been lying on the seat beside him, and in the accident it was lost. The horses had been spooked, and they'd run quite a distance. Debris from the carriage was scattered along the road for a mile or more."

Shannon shook her head, more mystified than before. "Then how did you happen to come across the contract?"

"I found it in the eyrie," Adam replied, and Shannon felt her jaw drop with surprise. "A year after the nest was abandoned," he went on, "I climbed up to it and there was Noah's copy! It was still wrapped in the oilcloth and it was buried under layers of sticks and grass, but it hadn't fared nearly as well as Liam's copy. It was in such bad shape that most of it is impossible to decipher. It was years before I appreciated its significance. I kept it mainly as a souvenir."

He chuckled at Shannon's expression. "Your eyes are as big and round as saucers, and I can see you're wondering how the eagles wound up with the contract, but I assure you that it's not as unusual as it seems. The only weird thing about it is that I should have been the one to recover it.

"You see, Shannon, every year at mating time the resident birds expand the nest. They use good-size limbs to enlarge the platform, then they line it with dry grass and other vegetation, I suppose to soften it for the nestlings. I found several scraps of fabric in the nest, and I also found a candle and a plastic detergent bottle. And the ankh."

The last had been added as an afterthought, and almost reflexively Shannon slid her hand inside the rolled collar of Adam's sweater and over the smoothly muscled column of his neck until her fingers contacted the hardness of the silver chain. The medallion might look cold, but it was warmed by his skin and it no longer had the power to arouse her resentment.

Smiling unconcernedly at Adam, she inquired, "When did you first recognize the value of the contract?"

"That would have been when I was in college." Adam turned onto his side so that he was facing her, propping his head with one hand. "Do you remember how we first met?"

Shannon nodded dreamily. "I'll never forget it."

"Since the deed had never been recorded, I wasn't sure how much legal status the agreement would have more than a century after the fact." He smiled wryly. "When you consider the improvements that have been made to the property over the years, and the fact that the MacLeods paid the taxes on it all that time, it probably

183

wouldn't have had much status of any kind. But when I came to see Dennis the night we met, I intended to appeal to his sense of justice. I was prepared to use the agreement as a *moral* weapon in order to force him to meet with my father and negotiate a merger."

"You didn't, though," Shannon reminded him softly.

"No, I didn't." He raised her hand to his lips and pressed a kiss in the palm. "And if it took a long time before I admitted why I hadn't carried out my plan, it's because I was dismayed to find I'd been bewitched by a fifteen-year-old enchantress who had no idea of her own charms."

"Thank you, kind sir." Smiling impudently, Shannon flirted Adam from beneath her lashes until another question occurred to her. "What about Liam's copy of the contract?" she asked. "Where was it all these years?"

"I hate to be the one to say it, Shannon," Adam replied dryly, "but Liam was less than honest. He must have bought off the witnesses and hidden the agreement away so that no one else learned about it until the original MacLeod house was being demolished. That was when Agatha found it, squirreled away in the walls. For a while she didn't know what to do about the situation. Then she came to me."

"She must have been amazed to find you already knew about the sale."

"She was," Adam said evenly, "and when she discovered I had my own copy and hadn't tried to use it against Dennis, that convinced her I love you. At our first meeting we reached a truce, but she was deeply distressed because Liam's nefarious actions offended her code of ethics, so she came up with what she thought was an equitable solution." He grinned. "I hope you agree that it's in your favor."

"Oh, I do! I find it extremely favorable!"

A carefree bubble of laughter escaped her. Her wild-honey hair was tumbled about her shoulders, her eyes were sparkling, her cheeks were vivid with the cold, and looking at Shannon, Adam felt the flaring heat of desire for her.

He cupped her cheek with one hand and leaned toward her until their lips met, parting sensuously so that his tongue could savor the sweetness of her mouth. Her arms looped about his neck and, impatient for the touch of her, he released the toggle buttons on her coat, lowered the zipper-fastener of her sweater over her breasts, and slid his hand inside to fondle the naked, rounded warmth within. Her heartbeat accelerated and her body responded under his touch, her nipples tingling from the chill of his hand and blooming with desire, and his fingers moved over her ardently, loving the feel of her.

When the kiss ended, they were both trembling, but not from the cold. His arms enfolded her and drew her near, and he rubbed his chin against her temple while she buried her face in the curve of his neck.

"Yesterday you asked what I expect of you," Adam said roughly, "and now I'd like to tell you. I want to teach you to like surprises again. I want you to share my bed and my life. I want us to watch our children grow up and have children of their own. But most of all, I want to love you and I want you to love me."

"Oh, Adam, I do love you," Shannon cried, her voice tremulous with emotion. "I've loved you from the first moment I saw you, and I want all those things too. But there's one more thing I'd like."

"What's that?" he asked softly.

Tilting her head back, she brought her mouth close to his ear and whispered her answer. In response the circle of Adam's arms tightened until he was hugging her with bonecrushing intensity. "Shameless hussy!" he reproached her, chuckling delightedly at her boldness as he proceeded to grant her wish, beginning by undoing the button at the waistband of her slacks.

"Adam!" She laughed shakily. "Not here!" He was tugging the slacks down over her hips, and she shivered as the icy air struck the naked skin of her stomach. "What if someone comes?"

"No one will," said Adam, still chuckling.

"Your father might. He told me he takes a walk by the river every day."

"Dad's tied up in a meeting."

To distract him, Shannon started tickling him, running her fingers along his ribs, making him laugh and try to stop her hands. In retaliation Adam began teasing and tickling her until she was laughing as helplessly as he was. Between giggles she asked, "What if his meeting breaks up early?"

"Simple." He sobered and kissed her on the lips to stop her laughter. "If anyone comes along," he murmured against her mouth, "we'll just tell them we're bird-watching."

All at once neither of them was laughing and his hands were moving over her insistently. At first she was cold, then his body was warming hers and she wasn't cold at all. Blanketed by the heat and hardness of his body, she forgot about the chill hardness of the ground at her back. In the rapture of his possession she was lifted out of herself until she was soaring, flying closer and closer to the sun. And when it was over and Adam had guided her safely back to earth, he chuckled again and murmured, "Gosh, Shannon, bird-watching was never this much fun before. We'll have to do it often."

He restored her clothing and his own and helped her to her feet, but he kept one arm around her shoulders, tucking her close to his side.

"The eagles have one more ritual I'd like to tell you about." As he spoke Adam reached out and broke a twig from one of the pine trees that had sheltered them. "As a final step when the courting is done and the eyrie is ready, one of the parents brings an evergreen sprig to the nest. I don't know if it serves some practical purpose or if it's purely decorative, but the sprig of greenery is always there."

Smiling, he touched the twig to his mouth and handed it to Shannon.

They started to climb the hill, and Adam filled her awareness until she saw him with deeper understanding. She had learned about much more than Noah and Liam and the eagles during the time spent by the nesting tree. She had learned about Adam and herself as well. She had learned that she loved Adam as he was, for what he was, and that even if she could change him, she wouldn't want to.

Adam's nature like the eagle's was to be free, and he would resist unnecessary shackles. Now and again he might leave her to travel to some faraway place, but he was bound to her by ties that were more powerful than mere chains, more potent than a million silver talismans. He would always return to her, and that was all that mattered.

As she walked Shannon brushed the pine branch

against her own lips and breathed in its heady fragrance. After a bit they took a shortcut that forked away from the main trail, and they had to go single file. When Adam turned back to help her on the climb, she smiled at him. She couldn't seem to stop smiling.

His eyes were shining with tenderness as he looked down at her, and she knew that never again would she fear his free spirit, never again would she feel threatened by the ankh and what it represented to him, for Adam had given her his pledge of love. He had given her the undying promise of the sprig of greenery.

LOOK FOR NEXT MONTH'S
CANDLELIGHT ECSTASY ROMANCES™:

Love—the way you want it!

Candlelight Romances

A love forged by destiny—
A passion born of flame

FLAMES
OF
DESIRE

by Vanessa Royall

Selena MacPherson, a proud princess of ancient
Scotland, had never met a man who did not desire
her. From the moment she met Royce Campbell at
an Edinburgh ball, Selena knew the burning
ecstasy that was to seal her fate through all eternity.
She sought him on the high seas, in India, and
finally in a young America raging in the
birth-throes of freedom, where destiny was bound
to fulfill its promise. . . .

A DELL BOOK $2.95

Danielle Steel
SUMMER'S END

author of *The Promise*
and *Season of Passion*

As the wife of handsome, successful, international lawyer Marc Edouard Duras, Deanna had a beautiful home, diamonds and elegant dinners. But her husband was traveling between the glamorous capitals of the business world, and all summer Deanna would be alone. Until Ben Thomas found her—and laughter and love took them both by surprise.

A Dell Book $3.50